THE MIDNIGHT LIBRARY

—

I CAN SEE YOU

DAMIEN GRAVES

SCHOLASTIC INC.

New York Toronto London Auckland Sydney
Mexico City New Delhi Hong Kong Buenos Aires

SPECIAL THANKS TO
SHAUN HUTSON

—

No part of this publication may be reproduced, stored in a retrieval system, or transmitted in any form or by any means, electronic, mechanical, photo-copying, recording, or otherwise, without written permission of the publisher. For information regarding permission, write to Scholastic Inc., Attention: Permissions Department, 557 Broadway, New York, NY 10012.

ISBN-13: 978-0-439-89394-7
ISBN-10: 0-439-89394-1

Series created by Working Partners Ltd.
Text copyright © 2006 by Working Partners Ltd.
Interior illustrations copyright © 2006 by David McDougall

12 11 10 9 8 7 6 5 4 3 2   7 8 9 10 11 12/0

Printed in the U.S.A.
First printing, November 2007

Welcome, reader.

My name is Damien Graves,
curator of that secret
institution:

The Midnight Library.

Where is The Midnight Library, you ask?
Why have you never heard of it?
For the sake of your own safety, these questions are better left
unanswered. However . . . as long as you promise not to reveal
where you heard the following (no matter who or *what*
demands it of you), I will reveal what I
keep here in my ancient vaults.
After many years of searching,
I have gathered the most terrifying
collection of stories known to
humanity. They will chill you to
your very core, and make
the flesh creep on your young,
brittle bones. So go ahead, brave
soul. Turn the page. After all, what's
the worst that could happen . . . ?

Damien Graves

LOOKING FOR DAYLIGHT? KEEP DREAMING.
THE MIDNIGHT LIBRARY CONTINUES....

———

VOICES

BLOOD AND SAND

END GAME

THE CAT LADY

LIAR

SHUT YOUR MOUTH

I CAN SEE YOU

THE DEADLY CATCH

THE
MIDNIGHT LIBRARY:
VOLUME VII

Stories by Shaun Hutson

—

CONTENTS

I CAN SEE YOU

Where *is everyone?* Michael Lewis wondered as he pedaled his bike down the road. He'd left his family's new home in the country nearly ten minutes ago, but during that time he'd seen only one vehicle on the road. A tractor had pulled out from a dirt track onto one of the narrow roads that snaked through the fields and hills around the farm. Other than that, Michael hadn't even seen another bike since he left the house.

The contrast with his journey to school in the city couldn't have been more obvious. Back there, he spent most of the ride dodging cars, buses, and taxis. Out here, it seemed, he had the road to himself.

Maybe no one leaves the house on a Monday morning out here in the countryside, he thought. He was still thinking about that when he swung his bike around a sharp bend and saw a car coming the other way. Michael smiled, almost relieved to see that someone other than himself was on the move.

The driver of the car waved happily at Michael as he passed, and Michael nodded back, remembering that the tractor driver he'd seen had also waved. People were certainly friendly here. As he continued cycling, he glanced to his left and saw a horse peering over the hedge at him. Michael grinned at the watching animal, wondering whether it was going to wave at him, too.

Still smiling broadly, he guided his bike around another bend in the road and down a steep hill. As he approached the school, Michael could see students of all ages moving around in the playground and on the sports field. Some were in groups, others wandered around in pairs. It didn't look as though anyone was on their own.

Michael felt a pang of nervousness as he realized that he wasn't going to know anyone. Still, the friendly waves he'd received on the way to school had to be a good sign, he figured. Hopefully the kids would be friendly, too.

He brought his bike to a halt, noting that several of the other students were eyeing him with curiosity. Michael chained his bike to the metal rack in the playground, hoisted his backpack onto his back, and wandered across the asphalt, looking around. Away to his right, some boys were playing a noisy game of soccer. To his left, three girls stared at him and giggled as he passed. He headed for the school playing field, feeling more than a little nervous at the prospect of his first day at his new school.

Then, suddenly, a tennis ball landed at his feet. Michael looked up to see where it had come from.

"Over here," a voice called, and Michael turned around to see a tall boy jogging toward him, followed by a group of shorter boys.

Michael stooped to retrieve the tennis ball and throw it back but, by that time, the little group was right next to him. The tall boy held out his hand, and Michael dropped the tennis ball into his outstretched palm.

"Are you the new boy?" one of the other boys said.

Michael nodded. "Yes," he said, smiling. "My name's Michael."

"Where did you live before you moved here?" another asked.

"The city," Michael told him.

"Aren't you living at Axby Farm?" the first boy went on.

Michael nodded again.

"So where did you park your bulldozer?" The question had come from the tallest of the boys. "Isn't that why you and your family are here?" he continued coldly. "To flatten the countryside and build a shopping mall?"

"No," Michael said. It was true that his father was a real estate developer and, in fact, Michael knew he had bought Axby Farm with the original intention of developing a shopping mall on the site. But then Mr. Lewis fell in love with the place and decided to move the whole family there instead. There would be no shopping mall anytime soon. "But it might not be a bad idea," Michael added, jokingly. "It looks as if you could use one out here."

This did not go over well. The tall boy took an angry step toward Michael, who wondered if he was about to create some kind of world record for getting into a fight quicker than anyone else ever had on their first day at a new school.

In fact, the boy prodded Michael in the chest with one finger. "See you later, city boy," he said. Then he turned around and sauntered away, the others bounding along behind him like hyenas following a lion.

Michael breathed a sigh of relief.

"I don't think the joke about the shopping mall was such a good idea, do you?" said a voice nearby. "It *was* a joke, wasn't it?"

"Yes," Michael replied, turning to see a girl with long, tangled hair and a broad grin.

"Don't worry about them," she advised. "They'll get over it."

"Thanks for that," Michael said. "I was maybe a *little* worried."

"Andrew Scuttle can be a bully," she continued. "He's the tall one. The others are like his posse, but they're OK when Andrew's not around."

"Posse. Now that's not a word I expected to hear outside the city," Michael said with a grin.

"Just because we live in the country doesn't mean we're backward, you know," the girl said, smiling at him. "My name's Stephanie, by the way. You're Michael, aren't you? Miss Hamilton told us last week you'd be joining our class."

"Did she tell you my dad was going to bulldoze all your houses and build a shopping mall out here, too?" Michael had to ask. "Is that why King Kong over there was waiting for me?"

Stephanie laughed and shook her head. "There have been stories in the local paper for months about a developer buying up land for a shopping mall," she explained. "People around here aren't too excited about the idea. They figure we've managed this long without one, so we don't need one now."

"But where do you go shopping?" Michael asked.

"There are stores and a market in the village," Stephanie replied. "And more stores in Wakely. That's about seven miles from here. There's a movie theater there, too, if you need something to do."

"I've got plenty to do at the moment helping my mom and dad clean up the farm," Michael said. He grinned ruefully. "Unfortunately."

"So your family's moved into Axby Farm, huh?"

"Did your teacher tell you that as well?" Michael asked.

"No, my dad did. And it was reported in the local paper that Axby Farm had been sold," Stephanie told him.

"Do they report on every house that's sold?"

"No. But no one's lived at Axby Farm for years! Everyone thought it was going to be replaced by the shopping mall. I think most people were relieved when they heard that a family had moved in."

"Everyone except Andrew over there," Michael murmured.

"I told you," Stephanie said. "Ignore him. Not all of us are like that."

"I'm glad you're not," he said with a smile. "I was wondering when I was going to see a friendly face."

Stephanie smiled back and motioned for him to follow her as the school bell sounded. "I'll show you where Miss Hamilton's classroom is," she told him. "And I promise not to chew hay or talk about pig breeding all through today's lessons, OK?"

"Cool," Michael said, laughing as he followed her through the main doors into school.

Michael put down his pen and looked around the classroom. He felt less nervous now, despite his potentially hazardous start to the day. He glanced across at Stephanie. She had really helped him settle in to his new school. His new teacher had turned out to be nice, too, and the essay on Amazon rain forests that she had assigned wasn't difficult. In fact, Michael found that he'd finished before most of the others.

He sat back and looked around the room. At the desk next to him, Stephanie was still writing, stopping occasionally to consult her textbook.

Miss Hamilton got up from her desk. "Continue working," she said. "I have to go get some books from the library. I'll be back in a few minutes." She left, closing the door behind her.

A vague murmur of chatter arose from the class. Michael grinned. This wasn't anything like his old school. If a teacher left her class there, the whole place immediately erupted with shouting and laughing. Obviously, Michael decided, his new schoolmates were better behaved. He listened to a couple of boys in front of him telling another about a recent fishing trip.

"Yeah, it was great," one boy was saying. "I got a perch, and Tom caught some sticklebacks."

Fishing? Sitting beside some water with a worm on a hook didn't sound very exciting to Michael. *Is that their idea of fun?* he wondered. *Maybe they watch cows grazing when they want something really exciting to do!*

He was relieved when lunchtime finally arrived, and he, like the rest of the school, marched out to the playground again.

"Come on, city boy," Stephanie said, coming up behind Michael and tugging his arm. "You can sit with me for lunch."

Michael nodded and followed her around to the steps of the main building. They both sat down and pulled their lunch bags out of their backpacks. Michael bit into his sandwich and gazed around the playground.

"Having fun?" Stephanie asked.

"Do you ever get bored living in the country?" Michael countered.

"Why should I? There's plenty to do."

"Like what? Fishing?" he asked. "Walking? When I go out, I see fields. That's it, just fields and nothing else. Back home, I could kick a soccer ball against a wall. Here, if I kick a ball, I end up chasing after it for miles — and stepping in about ten cow patties on the way!"

Stephanie laughed. "Sorry, Michael," she said, smiling. "It's going to take you a while to get used to living around here, that's all. What did you do for fun back in the city?"

Michael shrugged. "I don't know — loads of things. We'd go to the movies or hang out at the arcade. There was just so much more to do."

"You can do all those things here, too, you know," Stephanie told him. "All you have to do is get on a bus first. It's not such a big deal. You're telling me that everything was within two minutes' walk of your apartment?"

Michael shook his head. "No, it wasn't, you're right," he conceded. "So how do you spend your weekends?"

"I hang out with my friends, play with my little brother, listen to my iPod, stuff like that."

"You have an iPod?"

"And an Xbox. And a DVD player. We've even got running water, you know," Stephanie said, laughing.

"I know that," Michael grunted as she punched him playfully on the arm. "I just had the wrong impression of the country and the people who live here. Sorry."

"Don't worry about it," she told him. "In another six months, you'll have forgotten you ever lived anywhere else!"

"Yeah, you never know, I might even take up fishing," Michael said, grinning.

As Michael trudged along through the fields, he looked at the shopping list his mom had given him and wondered what his old friends were doing this Saturday morning. *Probably still in bed*, he thought, since it was barely nine o'clock.

He was pretty sure that none of them would be out running errands. Even if they were, it wouldn't involve a long walk to some village market to buy fresh fruit. Michael shook his head. His mom had decided that she wanted to make jam! She'd never made jam in her life before they'd moved to Axby Farm. His parents were enjoying the country life way too much.

Michael stuck his hand into his pocket and pulled out his cell phone. He hadn't been able to get a signal anywhere since they'd moved to the farm. Now, as he stood on one of the hills that overlooked the farmhouse, he wondered if the reception might be better.

He dialed his friend Matt and waited hopefully. When the word CALLING appeared on the screen, Michael nearly shouted for joy. Instead, he pressed the phone to his ear.

"Hello," said a familiar voice.

"Matt," said Michael, excitedly. "It's me, Mike Lewis."

"Mike!" Matt exclaimed. "Hey, buddy, I . . . ever . . . you . . ." His voice was cutting in and out, making it hard for Michael to make heads or tails of what he was saying.

"Matt, can you hear me?" Michael shouted into the phone. There was no reply. Michael cursed and scrambled farther up the hill in hopes of getting better reception.

"Matt, are you still there?" he tried again.

Silence.

Michael took the cell phone away from his ear to look at the screen. It had disconnected. And now the signal strength was weak. He sighed and shoved the cell phone back into his pocket.

He looked around to see that he was now up to his waist in tall, waving grass. He'd been so intent on his attempts to reach his friend that he hadn't noticed he'd strayed off the footpath. He forged ahead toward a line of trees at the top of the hill, feeling like an explorer making his way through the jungle.

When he finally reached the hilltop, he was impressed by the view. Looking back the way he'd come, Michael could see all of Axby Farm spread out below him. The farmhouse itself was nestled in the valley below and slightly to his right. About half a mile in front of the farmhouse, stretching away to his left, was a large beech tree forest. And on the far side of the farmhouse was another hill, topped by a single towering oak tree.

Michael turned to look at the view in the other direction. At the base of the hill, a small river curled away like a silver ribbon. He remembered his father saying that it was called Beech Creek and that it formed the western boundary of Axby Farm. A wooden bridge led across the river toward a tiny church. And on the other side of that was his destination — the village.

Michael ran down the hill and over the bridge to the churchyard. He had no idea how old the church itself was but, from the look of its weather-beaten stonework, he guessed it had to be at least two hundred years old — possibly more. The churchyard was surrounded by a low stone wall that he was just about to climb over when he noticed a wooden gate that led inside.

He hurried over to the gate and walked in. The graveyard was tangled and overgrown, the headstones crumbling like rotten teeth. Many were tilted at impossible angles, and some had fallen over long ago and were now covered in moss. Michael moved close to one and tried to read the inscription on the weathered stone.

"Frances Hutchens," he murmured. "Born 1795. Died 1831."

He moved on to the next headstone. He couldn't make out the name, but the date of the occupant's death was visible as 1849.

"What are you doing?" a voice hissed suddenly.

Michael spun around in surprise, his heart hammering against his ribs, and promptly tripped over a gravestone. He went flying to the ground, landing with a thud in the long grass. From his new position, he could see Stephanie peeping out from behind a tombstone.

"Stephanie!" Michael exclaimed, struggling to his feet. "You almost scared me to death! What are you doing?"

"I'm playing hide-and-seek with my little brother," Stephanie told him, grabbing his sweatshirt and pulling him back down into the grass. "Now keep quiet or he'll hear us."

Michael nodded and moved farther behind the gravestone with Stephanie.

"What were *you* doing, anyway?" Stephanie continued, lowering her voice.

"I just stopped to read the gravestones. I'm on my way to the store to get some stuff for my mom,"

Michael explained. "By the way, I tried to call one of my friends —"

"Shhhh!" Stephanie interrupted, pressing a finger to her lips. "I told you, I don't want Jack to find me. You can play, too, if you like."

"Wow, thanks!" Michael said, trying to sound enthusiastic.

"Well, would you rather be shopping for your mom?" Stephanie asked.

"Yeah, all right then, point taken," Michael said, grinning and lowering his voice. "I can't get a decent signal on my phone around here," he went on, "which is really annoying because I want to call one of my friends back in the city."

"Do you want to tell him about your new home?" Stephanie smiled. "Are you going to mention that you nearly woke up Farmer Axby?"

Michael looked puzzled, and Stephanie nodded in the direction of the gravestone he'd tripped over.

"'George Joseph Axby,'" Michael read. "'Born 1864. Died 1907. May he find peace in death.' This is Farmer Axby's grave!"

"Yup, the grave of the man whose house you're living in," Stephanie told him. "Haven't you heard the story of Farmer Axby? It's well known around here."

"I thought no one had lived at Axby Farm for about a hundred years," Michael said.

"They haven't," Stephanie confirmed. "Not for any length of time, at least. Farmer Axby and his family were the last ones. Other people have tried to move in over the years, but they've never stayed. They say that strange lights in the night and the smell of burning embers has driven away everyone. Noticed anything like that since you moved in?" she asked brightly.

Michael shook his head. "No, and I hope I don't!" he said vehemently. "So, keep going. What happened to Farmer Axby?"

"Well, he was a mean, grumpy old man," Stephanie explained, "but he got even worse when his wife left him, taking their two children with her. According to local legend," she went on, whispering softly, "Farmer Axby used to sit at his bedroom window every night just staring into the darkness, waiting for his family to come back. Sitting there all those nights drove him mad, and he started imagining that he could actually *see* his wife and children coming back to him across the fields. One night, he was so sure he'd seen them that he grabbed a lantern, put on his nice wool coat, and rushed outside. He ran back and forth in the darkness calling out, 'I can see you,' but he couldn't, of course, because they weren't there. He was out there for hours, shouting and screaming. Finally, he must have stumbled and dropped the lantern, because it came apart and set fire to the trees, the field, everything. The next day, nobody found a single trace of him — except for the broken lantern and a charred winter coat."

Michael swallowed hard. "So nobody ever found out if he survived?"

"No one knows for sure. They say that he kept screaming, 'I can see you,' all through the night," Stephanie said with a shudder. "And some people say that, on certain nights, you can *still* smell something burning in the hills where he died."

"Yeah, right," Michael said dismissively.

Stephanie shrugged. "I'm only telling you the story," she said.

Michael frowned then shook his head. "It's just some local superstition," he grunted.

"Maybe," she mused. "But you'd better not upset Farmer Axby. You don't want him to come looking for you, city boy."

"Very funny, Stephanie," Michael said, rolling his eyes. But he looked warily at the gravestone that had tripped him up.

"Got you!" declared a triumphant voice, making them both jump.

Michael got to his feet and turned to see a smiling little boy with bright red hair standing behind him.

"Jack." Stephanie laughed, getting up, too.

"I knew . . . I'd find . . . you," the little kid said breathlessly. He looked curiously at Michael.

"Michael, this is my brother," Stephanie announced, pointing at the boy who was now reaching into his jeans pocket for what Michael saw was an inhaler. "Jack, this is Michael, the new boy."

"I've got asthma," Jack said almost proudly, drawing a breath on the inhaler.

Michael nodded.

"It's my turn to hide now," Jack said, bouncing up and down.

"Do you want to stay and play with us?" Stephanie asked.

"No, thanks," Michael said. "I'd better get to the store and get that stuff for my mom. Next time I'll stay," he promised.

"Are you going to play I Can See You?" Jack demanded as Michael was about to leave.

Michael turned back, looking puzzled.

"It's a version of hide-and-seek," Stephanie explained. "We all play — all the kids from the village. Every September twenty-second, the anniversary of Farmer Axby's death, we come out into the fields around Axby Farm after dark and try to find one another. It's a lot of fun. It might be good for you to play, Michael. It'll help you get to know some of the other kids from school. If they see you joining in on one of our games, they might not think of you as so much of an outsider."

Michael nodded. "September twenty-second?" he muttered. "That's tomorrow night."

"So you're up for it?" Stephanie asked. "It's even more special this year because it's the hundredth anniversary of Farmer Axby's death."

"All right, I guess," Michael agreed, nodding.

"Jack and I will come get you at eight."

"OK," Michael said happily, making his way out of the graveyard.

"And, Michael," Stephanie called. "Don't forget to bring a flashlight."

The others have been talking about it at school all week, Dad," Michael said, chewing another mouthful of his dinner. From his seat at the table in the cozy farmhouse kitchen, Michael glanced at the window. It was dark outside and a harsh wind had picked up, whipping across the fields and whistling around the house itself until the windows rattled in their frames.

"They must really love hide-and-seek around here," his mom offered. "When I drove into the village this afternoon, the lady who runs the post office mentioned it. Her daughter's playing. It seems as if the whole village looks on it as some kind of special event."

"They do," Michael said. "Is it all right if I join in?"

"I don't see why not," his dad remarked.

"It just seems a little bizarre, playing a game to celebrate such a tragic event," his mom commented. "Besides, are you sure you want to be wandering in those fields at all hours of the night?"

"Sure," Michael said. "Anyway, it's not a celebration. It's just the locals' way of remembering Farmer Axby. And you don't have to worry about me, Mom. I'm thirteen, you know, not six. Besides, you were the ones who said I should get involved in local things."

"As a matter of fact, I was talking to Stephanie's dad about it today," Mr. Lewis added. "He wanted to warn me that tomorrow night we're going to have most of the kids from the village running across our land, trying to find one another in the dark. He said he used to play the same game when he was a kid. I don't think there's any harm in it."

Michael nodded. "It's only a game," he said, finishing his dinner and pushing away the plate.

The wind screamed around the house again. Outside in the yard, the door of the barn swung open on its creaky hinges and then slammed shut with a bang.

Oh, where is it?" Michael muttered irritably as he rummaged in another of the boxes of belongings stacked up in his bedroom, searching desperately for something that didn't seem to be there.

"What are you looking for, Mike?"

He turned to see his mom standing in the doorway, peering in at him.

"A flashlight," Michael told her. "Stephanie and Jack'll be here in ten minutes, and I can't find a flashlight. How am I going to play I Can See You without a flashlight?"

"Your dad's got one downstairs," his mom told him. "Use that for tonight."

Michael hurried out of the room and down to the kitchen.

"Dad!" he shouted excitedly. "Where's the flashlight? Can I borrow it for the game?"

"In the drawer next to the stove!" his dad called from the living room.

Michael found it immediately and flicked it on, pleased to see that it gave off a broad, bright beam.

"Are you all set now?" his dad said, entering the kitchen.

"Yes, I'm just waiting for Stephanie and Jack."

As if in response to Michael's words, there was a knock at the front door, and his dad headed off to answer it.

Seconds later, Stephanie and Jack wandered into the kitchen, both dressed in thick coats, hats, scarves, and gloves. Stephanie carried a flashlight. She shined it at Michael and laughed.

"Are you ready to go?" she asked.

Nodding his head, Michael threw on his coat, and they all headed out the front door.

"Just watch out for my boy, OK, Stephanie?" Michael's dad said, grinning. "I don't want him getting lost in the dark."

"Dad," Michael said through clenched teeth, "I'll be fine."

"I'll take care of him, Mr. Lewis," Stephanie said with a giggle. "Don't worry."

Then the trio headed out across the windy farmyard while Michael's dad waved cheerily from the warmth of the house.

"Why do parents have to be so embarrassing?" Michael muttered as he strode along.

"They can't help it," Stephanie said, shrugging her shoulders. "It's in their genes."

The three of them made their way down the dirt track that led from Axby Farm into the surrounding fields. Michael was struck by how dark the night truly was when there were no streetlights around. Several times, he stumbled on the uneven ground, barely able to see more than an arm's length in front of him.

"It's a good thing there's no moon tonight," Stephanie said. "That'll make the game even more exciting."

"I know," Michael muttered. "But if there was a moon, at least we'd be able to see where we're going. I can hardly see a thing!" He flicked on his flashlight, the beam cutting through the darkness.

"Don't turn that on yet," Stephanie told him.

"But we can walk faster when we can see the way."

"Yes, but if you keep it turned off, your eyes will get used to the dark, and you'll be able to see just fine before long," Stephanie explained patiently. "Trust me."

Michael nodded and switched off the flashlight again, trailing along behind Stephanie and Jack, who moved through the gloom and over the uneven land as easily as if they had night-vision goggles on.

They all climbed a low hill, the tall grass whipping at their legs in the wind, and Michael heard a strange clattering sound not too far ahead. Peering through the darkness, he realized that it was the sound of the wind rattling the branches of a large oak tree. It was the same tree that he had seen atop the hill when he had gazed out over the farm in daylight.

Michael was so busy staring at the oak tree that he almost tripped. He looked down to see what he had stumbled into in the blackness, but it was impossible to make out amid the long grass. As he raised his head, the blinding white glare of a flashlight made him wince. The light was being shined directly into his eyes.

"I didn't expect to see you tonight, city boy," said an all-too-familiar voice. It was Andrew Scuttle. He kept the flashlight aimed at Michael's face as he spoke.

Michael pulled his own flashlight from his pocket and shined it back at Andrew, who waited a moment before switching off his own.

In the beam of his own flashlight, Michael could see more kids from school and also several others from the village whom he didn't recognize. He guessed there must have been nearly thirty of them gathered on the overgrown slope, standing in a semicircle. He kept his flashlight leveled at Andrew for a moment longer, then switched it off when the beam flickered slightly.

"Listen, everybody," Andrew said, raising his voice to make himself heard above the howling wind. "It's September twenty-second, and you all know what that means. . . ."

Some of the group clapped and cheered.

"I think most of you have played before, but I'll explain the rules again, anyway," he continued, looking in Michael's direction. "When I give the signal, we all split up and everyone has ten minutes to find a good starting place. But you've got to stick to the land around Axby Farm, got it? So that means no farther than the woods to the north, this hill to the east, Beech Creek to the west, and the main road to the south."

There were murmurs of approval from the others.

"After ten minutes, we all start looking for one another in the dark," Andrew went on. "When you think you've found another player, you shine your flashlight at them and call out 'I can see you,' same as old Farmer Axby did all those years ago. Then you say the name of the person you've seen. Understand?"

The others nodded or muttered in agreement.

"The person who's been spotted must then stand still, with their flashlight switched on and shining at themselves — like this — to show that they're out of the game," Andrew explained. To illustrate his point, he flicked on his own flashlight and shined it upward from beneath his chin, momentarily illuminating his face. "The last player to be seen is the winner. Now, before we start, everyone check the batteries in their flashlight."

All over the hillside, beams of light cut through the blackness as the others did as they were instructed. Michael flicked on his own flashlight, muttering to himself as the beam faded and then went out completely. He pressed the switch again. This time, the light shined brightly for a couple of seconds but then turned to a weak yellow glow and died.

"You should have checked those batteries before you left home, city boy," Andrew said. He laughed smugly, throwing his own shiny red flashlight into the air and catching it again. Michael noticed that it looked brand-new — no risk of Andrew's flashlight running out of battery power!

"You can't play I Can See You when you can't see anyone, can you? It looks like you're out of the game. What a shame," sneered Andrew.

"It was fine earlier," Michael said irritably.

"It's no problem," Stephanie said, stepping closer. "You can team up with Jack and me."

"Do you mind?" Michael said, feeling sheepish.

She smiled and shook her head.

"OK, so Stephanie's going to babysit the city boy," scoffed Andrew. "You've already got your little brother with you, you know," he reminded her. "If there's three of you together, you've got no chance. You'll be spotted right away!"

"That's my problem," Stephanie said. "We'll still last longer than you, Andrew."

"You wish," Andrew said, smirking. "Ready, everyone?" he asked. "Check your watches. You've got ten minutes to find your starting places!"

Stephanie grabbed Michael's arm and tugged him away with her and Jack as all the others on the hillside also hurried away into the gloom.

"Stay close to me," Stephanie whispered. "We'll head past the big oak tree. There's an old, dried-up riverbed near there where we can hide."

Michael had to strain his ears to hear her over the gusts of strong wind. He was careful to stay close to Stephanie and Jack so that he could keep them in sight. With all the flashlights off, the night had closed in again, darker than ever, and though Michael could hear footsteps moving hurriedly in all directions, he could see no one but his own little group.

"I hope you know where you're going," Michael whispered after a moment.

"Shhhhh," Stephanie hissed at him over her shoulder, her breath clouding in the cold night air. "I know *exactly* where I'm going."

Michael shrugged and hurried after her through the darkness.

Suddenly, he almost fell over. His left foot had connected with what he could only imagine was a tree stump or a rock. It took all his efforts to remain upright.

He peered ahead and saw that Stephanie and Jack had climbed over a fallen tree and dropped into what looked like a shallow trench. Michael carefully scrambled over the tree trunk, too, and crouched down beside Stephanie.

"This is an old riverbed," she told him quietly. "It leads all the way from here across Axby Farm, as far as the woods to the north. It's a great way of getting around without the others seeing us. Even if they think they've heard something and they shine their flashlights this way, we only have to duck down and the beams will go right over our heads!"

"Cool!" said Jack, wheezing a little.

"Are you OK, Jack?" Stephanie asked. "Doesn't the cold air make your asthma worse?"

"I'm fine," Jack told her, waving his inhaler reassuringly under her nose.

"Super," said Stephanie, checking her watch. "This will be our starting place. The ten minutes are almost up. Everyone else will be on the move soon, looking for one another. So let's get going." She began to edge along the dry riverbed followed by her little brother. Michael brought up the rear.

Michael walked as quickly and quietly as he could manage, but the riverbed was full of dry leaves that rustled underfoot. Suddenly, there was a sharp *crack* as he stepped on a fallen twig.

Jack whipped around, and Stephanie glared at him. Michael grimaced and mouthed "Sorry" in the darkness. Then he looked around anxiously in case the sound had alerted anyone. The branches of the nearby oak tree rattled noisily as the wind continued to blow. Michael heaved a sigh of relief. He hoped that the noise would distract anyone listening.

"Come on," Stephanie whispered. "We need to keep moving."

The trio crept on. This time, Michael scanned the ground carefully to make sure he didn't step on anything else that could give away their position. He wondered where all the others were hiding.

Then he saw a shape move high up on the hillside. He was just about to touch Stephanie's shoulder and point it out to her when he realized that what he was looking at wasn't human. It moved like a fox, but it was really big, *too* big to be a fox, Michael decided. It had to be a stray dog.

He returned his attention to the game and scanned the area for other players. Up ahead, about a hundred yards away, he thought he could see the shadowy outlines of some of the others. However, as he, Stephanie, and Jack drew closer, Michael saw that the shapes were merely bushes, buffeted by the strong wind.

He realized he'd been holding his breath, so he let it out slowly. Just as he began to relax, he saw a bright beam of light shoot through the night.

"Get down!" Michael hissed urgently, and Stephanie and Jack dropped to their knees. Then they all peered over the edge of the riverbed, trying to find a face in the light.

"Look, someone's been found," Jack said quietly, pointing to a girl who was illuminating her own face.

"It's Simone." Stephanie chuckled. "I should have known! She's always the first to get caught." She turned to look at Jack and Michael. "We'll go and hide down by the old gate near the bottom of the hill for a while. This riverbed will take us right to it."

"I thought the idea was to find people," Michael pointed out.

"It is," Stephanie agreed. "But there's an old dirt trail that runs through the gate and loads of people use it. If we hide down there, we can catch people as they come by."

Michael grinned. "Good plan," he said approvingly.

As Stephanie and Jack set off, Michael glanced back for Simone, lit up by the flashlight. To his surprise, he saw nothing but darkness. No light. No figure. Nothing. Simone was no longer there.

Michael shrugged, wondering if her batteries had died like his own. Then he followed after Jack and Stephanie, pulling up the collar of his coat and shivering. The night seemed to be growing colder. The wind that had been blowing so ferociously at the start of the game had eased slightly now but, in its place, a freezing fog was beginning to form on the ground, swirling around Michael's legs in wispy clouds.

Just as Michael caught up with his friends, he heard movement nearby. It was definitely the sound of footsteps, and he could hear breathing, too. There was someone within just a few feet of them.

Quickly, he gestured to Stephanie and Jack, and all three of them froze, crouching low to the ground. Michael waited for the beam of light to shine on them, certain that whoever was nearby must have heard them, but no light broke the darkness, although Michael could still hear breathing. He guessed that the person must be getting his or her breath back while scanning the dark hillside for fellow competitors.

Stephanie reached back and tapped Michael on the shoulder, then touched her flashlight. Clearly she, too, had heard the breathing and planned to aim her flashlight at the other person. But she hesitated, and Michael could see that she was listening carefully, presumably wanting to be sure of where the person was.

Eventually, Stephanie smiled at Michael and nodded. She held up one finger, then two, then three. As she raised the third, she, Michael, and Jack sprang up from their hiding place, and Stephanie shined the flashlight in the direction of the breathing.

"I can see you, Jacob Williams!" Stephanie yelled gleefully as the flashlight cast a bright white light on the figure of a boy standing with his back to them.

The boy gasped in surprise and whirled around to face them. "Oh, no," he groaned, caught in the flashlight beam like a startled rabbit.

Michael, Stephanie, and Jack laughed.

"Turn on your flashlight, Jacob," Stephanie told him. "You're out."

Jacob nodded, switched on his own flashlight, and shined it under his chin. "I never even saw you," he moaned, shaking his head.

"That's the whole idea." Stephanie chuckled, switching off her own flashlight. "Now, don't tell anyone which direction we went, OK?"

Jacob shook his head sullenly, watching as the three of them crawled away in the darkness and the fog, hidden from view even more effectively by the bank of the ditch they were in.

Michael was smiling broadly as he, Stephanie, and Jack continued on their way. He was really beginning to enjoy the game, and he was suddenly curious about how many other people had been found. He paused and peered cautiously up over the edge of the ditch. Scattered across the fields, he could see the light from various flashlights, indicating that others had been caught. At least ten, he figured, counting the lights quickly.

Stephanie had been right. It was a good game, and the fact that they'd managed to stay undiscovered for what seemed like ages was making him feel even better. The prospect of winning really added to the excitement, and he wondered what Andrew would say at the end of the game if he got beaten by the "city boy." Michael crossed his fingers in the dark. He couldn't wait.

Unfortunately, he was so wrapped up in his thoughts of victory that he slipped on some fallen leaves and bumped into Stephanie, who promptly dropped her flashlight. It rolled away into the darkness.

Michael was about to scramble to his feet when Stephanie waved a hand frantically to indicate that he should stay down.

"There's someone there," Stephanie breathed. She pointed up at the side of the ditch and, even in the darkness and the gathering mist, Michael could see that there was someone standing there. Someone tall. Someone Michael was certain could only be Andrew.

"So zap him with the flashlight," Michael whispered back.

"I can't," Stephanie muttered. "I can't reach it." She pulled Jack closer to her and put her index finger to her lips as they all stayed still.

Andrew stood above them, looking around in the gloom. Michael figured he was probably listening for any sounds that would give away one of his competitors. Flat on his face in the ditch, Michael ached to get the flashlight and shine it on Andrew. At the same time, he knew that if he moved too much in an attempt to reach the flashlight, the dry leaves around him would instantly alert the other boy, and he didn't want that. Instead, Michael could only try to get more comfortable, pushing out one hand to lift himself out of the dirt.

As he did so, his fingers closed on something soft and he wondered what it was. It only took him a second to realize that it was a spiderweb. Even in the darkness, Michael could see the large spider emerge quickly from its lair in the ditch wall and crawl hastily out onto the web he'd disturbed.

Michael hated spiders. He watched it nervously, his heart thudding so hard against his ribs that he feared Andrew would hear it.

Stephanie looked down and saw the spider, too, but she merely pressed her finger against her lips again.

On the bank above them, Andrew still stood motionless, trying to hear or see figures moving through the black night and the silver mist.

Michael glanced at his companions. Jack was staring at the spider in fascination, while Stephanie was looking apprehensively from Michael's face to the spider and back again, clearly wondering whether Michael was going to give them away.

Michael definitely did not *want* to give away their position — especially not to Andrew of all people — but he knew that he was going to have to move soon. The spider was creeping slowly toward his outstretched fingers. Any moment now it would crawl onto his hand, and then Michael knew he would instinctively jump to get away from it.

At last, Andrew turned and walked away from the edge of the ditch. Michael breathed a sigh of relief, rolled away from the spider, and picked up Stephanie's flashlight. Then he scrambled to his feet and leaned against the other side of the riverbed, trying to catch his breath, waiting for his heart to stop pounding.

"I thought he was going to see us," Stephanie said quietly.

"So did I," Michael agreed. "But when I saw that spider, I didn't know what I was going to do."

"It was only a spider, Michael," Jack said, grinning.

Michael laughed and reached forward to ruffle Jack's hair. "You're a braver man than I am," he said with a smile.

"Come on," Stephanie whispered. "We'd better keep moving down to the bottom of the hill."

Michael nodded and was about to follow Stephanie when he glanced out over the top of the ditch and stopped in his tracks. "Wait a minute," he said, looking around in the darkness. "How long have we been playing?"

"About forty minutes," Stephanie told him. "Why?"

"We caught Jacob, right?" Michael said. "And you saw Simone get caught as well."

Stephanie nodded impatiently. "Yeah, so what?"

Michael motioned for Stephanie to look out across the fields. She straightened up and peered out into the night.

"Well, if people have been found," Michael asked, "why can't we see their flashlights? Wouldn't they still be standing where they were caught? But I can't see anyone!"

"We haven't heard anything, either," Jack pointed out.

"That could be because of the wind," Stephanie suggested. "I mean, Andrew was standing right above us and he never heard us, did he?"

"The wind isn't as strong as it was when we started, though, and we should still be able to see flashlights," Michael protested. "I think we should go back the way we came to see if the others are back there. What if everyone else has been found and the game's over or something?"

"No. Everyone stays where they are until the last

person's won," Stephanie insisted. "Those are the rules."

"So where are they, then?" Michael demanded. "Why can't we hear anybody?"

All three of them stood still, listening intently for the slightest sound.

"The wind's hardly blowing now," Michael insisted. "And yet we *still* can't hear them."

"That's because everyone's trying to be quiet so they don't get caught," Stephanie pointed out. "And the mist's thicker now. It's harder to see anything."

"Look, there," Jack said, pointing into the night.

Michael saw it — a dull yellowish light that gleamed on the other side of the field. It glowed for a second, then it was gone.

"Someone else is still playing," Stephanie insisted. "They must be. And we know Andrew is because we've just seen him."

"Well, let's go that way, then," Michael said, gesturing with the flashlight. "Maybe we can catch someone. . . ."

Stephanie hesitated for a moment, then she nodded. The three of them climbed cautiously up out of the ditch and set off across the dark field. Michael kept as low as he could and hoped the mist would hide him.

Now that the howling wind had died down, the silence that had replaced it was unnerving. Michael nervously glanced left and right as he walked, even though he could see very little in the impenetrable blackness.

The same yellow light flashed again, this time away to their left.

"Come on, let's head toward that light," Michael suggested. "At least we know someone must be over there."

Stephanie, who was leading the way, nodded and turned, but as she did so, she tripped and almost fell.

Michael shined the flashlight briefly at the ground to see what had caused her to stumble. It was a pair of yellow rubber boots.

Stephanie reached for one and held it up. "Can I have the flashlight for a moment?" she asked Michael, keeping her voice low.

He handed over the flashlight and Stephanie shined it inside the boot.

"I thought so. These are Simone's," Stephanie said, reading the name tag inside the boot. "But where is she?"

Michael shrugged and looked all around the field. There was nobody to be seen. "Maybe it's some kind of joke," he suggested.

"What's this?" Jack wanted to know. He was kneeling on the ground pointing at a pile of white dust close to the rubber boots.

Michael kneeled beside Jack and examined the dust, dipping one finger into the powdery substance. "It's ash," he said quietly, rubbing it between his fingers. "Like something's been burned."

"Simone got caught, so now she's trying to make it look like she's disappeared!" Stephanie said. "I tell you what, I bet she's hiding around here somewhere." And with that, Stephanie switched on the flashlight and swept the beam 360 degrees around them. "Come on, Simone," she said, smiling. "Show yourself!" But the flashlight merely revealed that the wispy, silvery mist was rapidly becoming a heavy, gray fog.

"What are you doing?" Michael snapped. "Someone will see us."

"That's what you want, isn't it?"

"No. I just want to know where everyone else is," Michael explained, feeling slightly uneasy.

"You must be right. This must be some kind of joke," Stephanie said. "That *has* to be why we can't see or hear anyone else. And it would explain Simone's boots. The others are probably just trying to scare us."

"Or scare *me*, you mean," Michael added, his temper ignited by his anxiety. "Is that the plan? Frighten the city boy? How do I know you're not in on this, too?"

Stephanie looked angrily at him. "How could you say that?" she snapped.

"I'm sorry. I didn't mean it," Michael apologized.

"You should know me better than that."

"I said I didn't mean it," Michael insisted. "I think we're all getting a little jumpy."

"I'm not," Jack said with an enthusiastic smile.

"Come on. Let's keep walking," Stephanie suggested, striding off through the thick grass.

Michael waited uncertainly for a moment, then realized that Stephanie had the flashlight. He would be completely lost if he found himself alone in the fog, so he set off after her. "Where are we going?" he asked. "Are you sure you still know where we are?"

"It's OK. Trust me," Stephanie told him.

"But how do you know we're going the right way?" Michael demanded.

"I just do," Stephanie said, sighing wearily.

"Well, are we heading back to my house, or back to where we all started playing?" Michael asked.

"Back to your house," Stephanie replied. "I'm bored with the game now."

"But my house is *that* way," Michael said, jabbing a finger off to his left.

"No it isn't," Stephanie protested. "I've lived here —"

"Oh, stop arguing," Jack interrupted. "We're lost, aren't we?"

All three of them stood still, the wind rising slightly and stirring the thick silver fog that surrounded them.

"Jack's right. We *are* lost, aren't we?" Michael echoed, looking at Stephanie.

Stephanie sighed. "Well, I *think* your house is this way," she said, and continued walking through the tangled grass.

Michael sighed and followed, and Jack hopped along behind, seemingly the least concerned of the trio.

It seemed to be growing colder by the second and, despite the fact that Michael was wearing a thick coat, a sweatshirt, and a T-shirt, he found that he was beginning to shiver. He forgot about that for a moment, though, when he stepped on something hard.

He dropped to his knees to retrieve the object. "Stephanie," he said quietly, holding what he'd found out in front of him. "Look at this."

Stephanie drew closer and peered at what Michael had in his hand. "It's a flashlight," she said, a note of puzzlement in her voice.

"It's Andrew's flashlight," Michael told her. "I remember seeing it." He flicked it on and off. "And it's still working."

"What are those?" Stephanie wanted to know, pointing at four indentations on one side of the flashlight's plastic grip. The marks made it look as if it had been squeezed by a powerful hand.

"The plastic looks . . . melted," Michael said, peering at the marks. "But what could have burned it like that?"

Stephanie shined the flashlight around, and something caught Michael's eye. On the ground, just where he'd picked up the flashlight, was more of the white ash they had found near Simone's rubber boots. Michael pointed to it.

Stephanie said nothing. She did, however, keep her own flashlight turned on.

"I thought you didn't want to lose the game," Michael said.

Stephanie smiled grimly. "I didn't, but I think you're right," she confessed. "Something weird's going on. Maybe it's just some stupid joke, but the game must have been called off. I think we should concentrate on getting back to your house now."

Michael nodded and switched on Andrew's shiny red flashlight. The bright beam cut reassuringly through the darkness, but fog still clouded the view ahead.

"Can I hold the flashlight?" Jack asked Michael hopefully.

Michael hesitated a moment, but then handed it over. Jack ran back and forth, waving the flashlight around.

"It won't take us long now," Stephanie said in a determined voice, and Michael wondered whether she was trying to reassure him and Jack — or herself.

They trekked onward, their route taking them up a hill, through some trees, and then down through another field. Michael's legs were aching, and he found himself breathing heavily. That made him think of Jack.

"You'd have thought all this excitement would have made Jack's asthma worse," he remarked to Stephanie. "But I haven't heard him wheezing for a while."

Stephanie stopped. "You're right," she agreed. "He has gotten very quiet. Are you all right, Jack?"

There was nothing but silence.

Stephanie turned a complete circle, shining her flashlight into the gloomy night. Michael followed the direction of the beam, but he could see nothing but grass and shadowy trees looming out of the fog.

Jack was gone.

"Jack!" Stephanie called frantically.

"Jack!" echoed Michael, cursing the fog that obscured their vision.

Stephanie swept the flashlight back and forth across the night-soaked countryside, but its powerful beam revealed nothing but trees, bushes, tangled grasses, and the ever-thickening fog.

Michael ran back up the slope they'd just descended. He could hear Stephanie following right behind him. "He must have wandered off without our realizing," Michael said, stopping and looking left and right for any sign of the boy.

"We've got to find him, Michael," Stephanie said anxiously, her eyes filling with tears.

"Don't worry. We'll find him," Michael assured her. "I promise you, we're not going anywhere until we have."

Stephanie wiped her eyes, still shining the flashlight over the ground. "Look! Over there," she gasped.

The flashlight was shining on something plastic in the grass. Stephanie and Michael ran toward it. But as soon as she saw what it was, Stephanie burst into tears.

It was Jack's inhaler. But the plastic was melted and, as with Andrew's flashlight and Simone's rubber boots, there was a thick coating of silvery gray ash all over the inhaler and on the ground around it.

"If he's lost this and he has an asthma attack, something awful could happen!" Stephanie sobbed in horror.

"It must have fallen out of his pocket when he was running," Michael said firmly. "Hang on to it, and we'll give it back to him when we find him."

Michael squinted through the night and saw a glimmer of yellow light about a hundred yards ahead. "Over there," he said, pointing toward the light.

"Jack!" Stephanie shouted, running toward the light. Michael followed her.

"Stay where you are, Jack," Stephanie panted.

"He must be using the flashlight to show us where he is," Michael said.

"Nearly there, Jack!" yelled Stephanie.

They were less than a hundred feet away when the light flickered and went out.

"Jack!" Stephanie screamed. "Put the flashlight back on!"

Michael ran on, pulling ahead of Stephanie as if they were in some kind of bizarre race. "I'll get him," he called over his shoulder. "Jack!" he shouted again, slowing down as he saw a wooden fence loom out of the fog in front of him.

He climbed up the fence, pausing as he reached the top. To his delight, he heard heavy, rasping breathing a short distance away to his right. "Jack," he gasped, a huge sense of relief sweeping through him.

Michael swung himself over the fence and dropped down on the other side. But immediately his foot slipped, and he felt himself tumbling, over and over, down a steep hill. Dizzy and gasping for breath by the time he reached the bottom, he struggled to his feet and began to haul himself back up the hill.

Before long, his legs were throbbing with the effort of the climb, but he had to keep going. When he reached the wooden fence, he realized he'd made it back to the top of the hill. However, he could no longer hear Jack's breathing. And, as he looked around, another thought struck him: *Where is Stephanie?*

He could see no beam of light, and he could hear no footsteps. First Simone, then Andrew, then Jack, now Stephanie! What was going on? Michael began to panic more than ever. He swallowed hard and tried

to make sense of the situation. Stephanie had probably followed him over the fence and slipped, just as
he had done.

Suddenly, an eerie howl echoed through the darkness. It sounded exactly like a wolf. Michael shivered
as he remembered the stray dog he had spotted earlier
in the evening. *Not a wolf,* he told himself firmly. *It's just
the stray dog from earlier — or maybe a fox.*

The darkness, the fog, and the strange events of the
night were making his imagination work overtime,
Michael realized. He leaned against the fence and
forced himself to calm down. Gradually, his pounding
heart slowed, and his breathing grew steady again.

And as it did so, Michael noticed that he could feel
a soft, woolen fabric beneath his fingers. He frowned
and peered at it in the darkness. It was Stephanie's
coat. It was caught on the fence, just hanging there,
as if Stephanie had simply slipped out of it and left
it behind.

"Stephanie!" Michael called frantically.

There was no response. But then, once again, he
heard that low, wheezy breathing that he'd heard
earlier. "Jack!" Michael yelled. "Stephanie! One of you,

answer me!" His voice seemed to echo in the night as if it was bouncing off the fog around him.

The low, rasping sound was now louder, closer to him. He spun around and smiled. There was a light less than fifty feet away! But the smile died on his lips as he realized that it wasn't coming from a flashlight. This light was flickery and golden like candlelight.

Now it was moving toward him, suspended at eye level. It drew closer still, getting brighter until the glare was so great that Michael had to shield his face and, all the time, the wheezing, rasping breathing grew louder. It reminded him of a growling dog.

"Is that you, Jack?" Michael whispered, his voice quavering.

The ball of light was only a few yards away now, and Michael could see it clearly at last. It was the glow of a lantern. The flickering flame cast a pool of dull light. And now, besides the rasping breaths, Michael became aware of something much worse: a terrible smell that caught in his nostrils and throat. It smelled like something was burning.

Michael tried to back up, but the wooden fence behind him blocked his way. Fear held his gaze to the light. And then the lantern was raised close to a face and, at last, Michael could see who was carrying it.

With the stink in his nostrils and the sound of that heavy breathing in his ears, he opened his mouth to scream, but no sound came out. All he could do was stare in horrified disbelief.

In front of him stood a man — or at least what had once been a man. Michael could just barely make out a blackened face and hands that were charred like a burned match. Instantly, he knew that he was looking at Farmer Axby.

Farmer Axby opened his mouth to reveal a hideous, bloated tongue. "I can see you, Michael Lewis," he rasped.

And in that split second, Michael realized why there had been only ashes where the other players should have been.

"I can see you," the undead farmer said again, and this time there was an unmistakable note of triumph in his voice. With one stinking breath, Farmer Axby blew out the lantern.

And there was only darkness.

PICTURE PERFECT

Keep climbing, Brandon, you're almost there!" Brandon Taylor heard his brother, Jake, shout encouragingly from down below. With one last, huge effort, Brandon heaved himself up onto the top of the high stone wall and sat astride it, peering down triumphantly at Jake.

He could see his identical twin standing with his hands on his hips, gazing up at him.

"Come on, slowpoke!" Brandon called down. He watched as Jake reached for the ladder and propped it against the wall, checking it was secure before beginning his own ascent.

"Why couldn't I have used the ladder, too?" Brandon asked as his brother reached the top of the wall.

"You said you could climb up by yourself," Jake reminded him, swinging a leg over so that he, too, was sitting safely astride the cold stone. "Anyway, I'm carrying all of this stuff, right?" He placed a can of black paint and two large brushes on top of the wall between them.

Brandon looked out across the garden that lay beyond the wall. "No wonder Grandaunt Lucy doesn't want anyone to see in here," he mused, gazing at the overgrown wilderness that stretched away before him. "It looks like she hasn't done any gardening in years!"

Jake nodded in agreement, also surveying the expanse of land.

Brandon looked down to the bottom of the wall. Beneath the two boys were several overgrown lilac bushes, their branches intertwined like battling squids. Ivy covered the wall where the boys sat, clinging to it like clutching fingers. Brandon rattled a length of it experimentally. It was tough and strong, he noted with approval. It could prove useful during the climb down.

Beyond the lilac bushes and untended flower beds, a large expanse of overgrown lawn stretched away toward a line of willow and poplar trees that hid the bottom part of the garden from the house itself.

The building was just visible through the branches of the trees. It was a huge old mansion that looked only slightly better cared for than the garden that surrounded it. Paint was peeling badly from the outside walls, the roof was clearly missing some shingles, and a nearby toolshed had pieces of reed sticking out of its thatched roof like badly combed hair.

"No wonder nobody ever comes here," Brandon said, dismissing the ivy and deciding to use the ladder to get down. He heaved it up from the outside of the wall and lowered it into the garden. "The house looks as bad as everything else."

"That's not why people don't come here, though," Jake pointed out. "It's because of Grandaunt Lucy. The kids in the neighborhood are scared of her."

"I'm not surprised. She's a miserable old witch."

"And rude," Jake added.

"And mean." Brandon said with a laugh.

"Too bad she's our grandaunt," Jake said with a sigh.

"Maybe if she spent more time talking to people instead of staring through that telescope of hers every night, more people would come and visit her," Brandon said, starting to climb down the ladder.

"By the time we've finished, she won't be spending much time looking out of that window," Jake said with a grin.

"At least, not unless she's got X-ray eyes and she can see through the paint we're going to use on the glass," Brandon agreed with a chuckle.

"I heard that she wasn't *always* as weird as she is now," Jake said. "She just went a little, well, bonkers, after her twin sister disappeared years ago."

"Where did her sister go?" Brandon asked curiously.

"No one knows, dummy. If they did, she wouldn't still be missing, would she?" Jake told him, laughing.

Brandon had to acknowledge the truth of that. He grinned. "Hey, tell you what, she probably just got fed up with Grandaunt Lucy and ran away," he said, jumping down from the ladder and landing in the tangled grass.

"Here, take the paint," Jake called, leaning forward and tossing the can carefully to Brandon.

Brandon caught it, then watched as Jake stuck the two paintbrushes in the back pocket of his jeans and quickly climbed down the ladder to join him.

Jake carried the ladder as the two of them set off across the lawn toward the line of trees. When they got there, they paused to check that the coast was clear. The house was close now, across another stretch of unmown lawn and a weed-infested gravel pathway.

Brandon checked for any sign of his grandaunt, then led the way over to the house. He passed a pond, its surface covered with thick green slime. It was surrounded by several statues, and he couldn't help noticing that one was missing its head.

Brandon stopped behind a large hydrangea bush that was growing close to the house. Jake almost bumped into him.

"So which room is the one with the telescope?" Jake wanted to know, peering up at the house from the cover of the bush.

"Shhh," Brandon warned. "Keep your voice down or she'll hear us coming." He pointed to one of the second-floor windows. "She keeps the telescope in that room up there, I think. But we'll do one or two of the others as well, just to make sure." He laughed. "She's going to think it's really dark outside when she looks through her telescope tonight. I wonder how long it'll take her to realize her windows are covered in black paint!"

Jake chuckled and pried the lid off the paint can while Brandon pushed the ladder up against the wall of the house.

Brandon took the paint can and a brush from Jake, then climbed the ladder. He peeped cautiously through the window to make sure Grandaunt Lucy wasn't in that very room, and then dipped the brush into the black paint.

"Go on," Jake urged impatiently. "I'll do the next one."

Brandon was about to press the brush to the glass when a loud yapping nearly made him fall off the ladder.

"Oh, no, I'd forgotten about Michelangelo!" said Jake as a small brown-and-white spaniel hurtled toward him.

Barking and growling, the little dog ran at Jake, who quickly climbed up the ladder behind Brandon.

"What are you doing?" Brandon demanded. "Get down!"

"I don't want to get bitten!" Jake explained, staying put.

"Grandaunt Lucy's got more teeth than that dog," Brandon told him. "Just go and pet him to calm him down — or else she might hear him barking."

"*You* calm him down," Jake said indignantly, staring down at the little dog that was still yapping excitedly up at the boys, its tail wagging furiously.

"Oh, just do it, Jake! We can't stay up here all day. Look, the spaniel likes you, its tail's wagging."

Slowly, Jake descended the ladder. "Good dog, Michelangelo," he said nervously. The dog stopped yapping and jumped up at Jake eagerly. Jake patted it gently on the head. Michelangelo bounced around Jake's legs in excitement — and bumped against the foot of the ladder.

The ladder shifted, and Brandon let out a cry of surprise and alarm as he wobbled uncertainly for a moment. "I'm going to fall!" he yelled.

As Jake tried to draw Michaelangelo away from the ladder, the little dog bumped into it once again. This time, Brandon clutched the windowsill to steady himself and dropped the paint can.

It fell to the ground and landed with a thud. Black paint sprayed in all directions, most of it over the patio, but some up the wall of the house. Several thick black blobs landed on Michaelangelo, who promptly squealed and fled around the side of the house yelping louder than ever.

"Uh-oh," said Jake, looking at the spreading puddle of black paint. "Let's get out of here. Quick!"

Brandon dropped the paintbrush and scrambled down the ladder as fast as he could, jumping the last three rungs. No sooner had he hit the ground than he heard an angry voice cutting through the warm summer air.

"What do you think you're doing?"

Grandaunt Lucy had appeared around one corner of the house, shaking her pudgy fist angrily at the boys. For an old lady, she moved with surprising speed.

"Run!" Brandon yelled, racing away from his grandaunt toward the front of the house, with Jake close on his heels.

"How dare you?" Grandaunt Lucy bellowed. The boys fled down the long gravel driveway in front of the giant house, then frantically climbed the gate. "You won't get away with this, you know!"

But the boys didn't stop. Glancing over his shoulder, Brandon saw that his grandaunt had given up the chase. Instead, she stood outside the house, with Michaelangelo leaping about her ankles, barking excitedly. "You'll be sorry!" she shouted after them furiously.

I can't believe you'd do something so stupid," Mr. Taylor snapped.

Brandon didn't know what to say. His dad was obviously not happy. Brandon looked hopefully at his brother, who was trailing along behind. Jake shrugged. Clearly, he didn't have any bright ideas or brilliant excuses, either.

"I mean, you're thirteen," their dad continued. "You're not little kids anymore."

"Dad, it was only intended to be a practical joke," Jake said sheepishly.

"A practical joke?" his dad snapped. "Vandalizing

your grandaunt's house is some kind of a joke to you two?"

"We didn't vandalize it, Dad," Brandon said. "And anyway, we were just going to paint a couple of the windows black."

"I know what you were going to do. Your grandaunt said she found the paint spilled all over the patio."

"Sorry, Dad," Brandon muttered, just as Jake said exactly the same thing.

"Well, that's not good enough this time," Mr. Taylor said. "I know you two can find trouble even when you're not looking for it, but this is disgraceful! You were trespassing on your grandaunt's property. You were going to paint over her windows. And as if that isn't bad enough, you could have hurt yourselves. You're lucky one of you didn't fall off that ladder! What you did was dangerous, irresponsible, and downright stupid. How on earth did you expect to get away with it? Did you think your own grandaunt wouldn't recognize you? She called me as soon as you two had run off."

"If it hadn't been for the dog —" Brandon began.

"You'd have painted over her windows!" Mr. Taylor interrupted. "You'd have had a good laugh and gotten away with it! And did you ever stop to think about how your grandaunt would have felt if your little prank had succeeded? Apart from her dog, she's all on her own in that big house with no one to talk to. She's just a lonely old lady who's been unhappy ever since her sister went missing when they were both ten. That was fifty-five years ago." Mr. Taylor sighed as they crossed the road that led toward Grandaunt Lucy's house. "Well, I'm going to let your grandaunt decide what you two can do to make this up to her. If I was her, I'd make you clean the entire house from top to bottom."

Jake groaned. "That'd take forever, Dad," he said. "I don't think that place has been dusted for about ten years!"

"That's because your grandaunt doesn't move around so well these days," said Mr. Taylor.

"She was moving quickly enough when she came running out of her house to chase us," Brandon remarked. Instantly, he wished he hadn't.

His dad glared at him, and Brandon bowed his head. He'd never seen his dad so angry before. "Sorry, Dad," he said again.

"You can apologize to your grandaunt," Mr. Taylor told them as he unlocked the gate into Grandaunt Lucy's driveway.

Brandon glanced at his brother and met Jake's gaze. He knew that Jake was dreading this as much as he was.

They stood, silent and uncomfortable, as their dad marched up to the front door and banged three times with the large, lion-headed brass knocker. Brandon thought that the face of the metal lion seemed to be leering mockingly at him.

After a moment or two, the door opened and Grandaunt Lucy looked out. She smiled at the boys' dad then looked at the twins and raised her eyebrows questioningly.

"Well, I've brought these two delinquents to see you," said Mr. Taylor. "They'd like to say sorry for their stupid prank earlier."

"Sorry," Brandon and Jake piped up together.

"And they'd like to do something to help you," Mr. Taylor continued. "Wouldn't you, boys?"

Brandon and Jake nodded unenthusiastically.

"So, whatever you want them to do, just let them

know and they'll get started right away," Mr. Taylor finished.

Grandaunt Lucy nodded. "Very well. Thank you," she said. "You'd better come inside, boys," she added, frostily.

As Brandon headed past his dad toward Grandaunt Lucy, Mr. Taylor bent to whisper in his ear. "I don't want to see you two back home until you've finished whatever job your grandaunt asks you to do," he said sharply. "Understand?"

"Yes, Dad," Brandon replied miserably.

As he entered the house, he heard his dad's feet crunching on the gravel as he stomped away.

Brandon watched apprehensively as Grandaunt Lucy shut the front door behind him. Then she ambled off toward a room on her left. He and Jake stayed put in the hall, gazing around warily.

"It's like a museum in here," Jake whispered. "It's even dustier than I remembered."

"Well, it must be a couple of years since we've been inside," Brandon reminded him.

"Come here, boys!" Grandaunt Lucy called. The

twins wandered unenthusiastically in the direction of her voice.

She was standing in front of a gigantic open fireplace in her living room. The room was huge — so huge that the high ceiling made the slightest noise echo and, when Grandaunt Lucy coughed, the sound seemed to bounce around the room like a tennis ball. Brandon noticed that inside the fireplace, instead of wood or coal, there was a metal container filled with flowers. Their scent filled the room with a sweet, cloying fragrance that made him feel slightly sick. Brandon looked down at his feet and noticed that the yellow carpet was worn so thin in places that the wooden floorboards beneath it were showing through.

The walls were festooned with European paintings of all kinds — from portraits to landscapes. The twins' mother was a history teacher, so Brandon was able to recognize one of them as the Battle of Waterloo. Cobwebs clung to most of the frames. But the paintings served a useful purpose: The walls behind them were a terrible mess. The plaster was chipped and, in a number of places, it had actually crumbled away from the wall entirely. Brandon could see some of it lying in the fireplace, looking like chunks of crushed meringue.

"Since I spoke to your father earlier, I have been trying to think of a job you can do for me," Grandaunt Lucy said. "I considered asking you to weed the garden or even clean the windows, but then I decided that, since you both seem to be so fond of painting, I would ask you to do some decorating for me."

Brandon and Jake exchanged a look of despair. If the rest of the house was anything like the living room, then Brandon didn't even want to imagine what kind of job was in store for them.

"Follow me," said Grandaunt Lucy, leading the way out into the hall. She paused to ensure that the boys were behind her and then began to climb the wide staircase.

There were more paintings on the walls that lined the stairs. Here they partially concealed poorly hung, discolored wallpaper that was covered in a hideous flowery pattern. The stairs creaked as they climbed, and dust swirled in the sunshine that streamed in through a large landing window.

There were six doors leading off the landing, one of which was down a short, dark hallway to the right. It was that door toward which Grandaunt Lucy led the boys. Brandon was struck by the fact that the door opened smoothly and easily, as if on well-oiled hinges. Given the neglected air of the rest of the house, he had been expecting a protesting squeak.

"In here," Grandaunt Lucy said, motioning them inside.

The room was empty. There wasn't even a carpet on the floor, just bare boards beneath their feet. The door swung smoothly shut behind them with the faintest sigh, and Brandon felt a breath of air on the back of his neck. He shivered uneasily.

"Did you feel that?" he asked Jake, glancing at his brother. "It was as if somebody just blew on the back of my neck."

Jake shrugged. Clearly, he'd felt nothing unusual. Brandon figured that he was letting his imagination run away with him in the creepy old house.

"I want you to strip the wallpaper," Grandaunt Lucy said. "As you can see, the room needs redecorating. It hasn't been touched for more than fifty years."

"No kidding," Brandon murmured.

"What did you say, Brandon?" his grandaunt asked sharply.

"Nothing, Grandaunt Lucy," he said quickly, giving her a bright smile.

"I'll go and find you what you need," she continued. "A bucket of warm water, some sponges, and some putty knives should get this paper down."

Both boys nodded as the old woman moved out of the room.

"I think a flamethrower might be more useful," Brandon remarked, looking at the lumpy, discolored paper that covered all four walls. It was deep red and traced with silver lines that rippled across it like glistening veins. He ran his fingers over it experimentally. It felt thick, more like fabric than paper. It also seemed to be pretty firmly attached to the wall.

"I wouldn't mind having Dad's steamer," Jake said, joining Brandon at the nearest wall. "That'd get it off more quickly than putty knives and hot water will." He prodded the wallpaper. "This stuff looks like it was put up with concrete."

Suddenly, the door of the room swung shut, and, again, Brandon heard what sounded like a faint sigh. A shiver ran swiftly up and down his spine. He turned around, but there was no one and nothing behind him, so he returned his attention to the wall.

"I could run home and get the steamer," Jake suggested. "Or should we try with the water and putty knives first?"

Brandon nodded without looking at his brother. He wasn't really listening. The wall fascinated him, and he was suddenly gripped by an enormous urge to see what lay behind the paper.

"Brandon," Jake persisted, "I said I could run —"

". . . home and get the steamer," Brandon finished for him. "Yes, I know. It's a good idea. Wait until she's brought the water and the rest of the stuff, and then you can sneak out and get it."

"How long do you suppose the paper's been up?" Jake asked.

"I don't know. A long time by the look of it."

He heard movement outside the door and turned to see Grandaunt Lucy coming in, carrying a bucket of water with two sponges floating in it. She took two putty knives from the pocket of her cardigan and handed one to each boy.

"There's a stepladder out on the landing," Grandaunt Lucy said. "You can use that to reach the tops of the walls."

Brandon nodded as his grandaunt frowned at him and left the room.

"I'll get started," Brandon said with a sigh, reaching for one of the sponges in the bucket. "You go get the steamer."

"OK," Jake said. "Back in a minute." And he hurried out, closing the door behind him.

Brandon pressed the wet sponge against a section of the wallpaper nearest to him, and he watched as the fluid ran down the paper. Then he picked at the edge of the wallpaper strip to see how easily it would come away from the wall. The paper peeled back slightly, and, as Brandon touched the wall behind it, he was surprised by how cold it felt. A chill ran through his fingers, up his arm, and down his back like some weird kind of frigid electric shock.

Once again, he heard the low whisper of a sigh that had signaled the opening and closing of the door. He looked around, expecting to see that Grandaunt Lucy had returned and readying himself to explain Jake's absence. But the door was closed.

When Jake got back to the room with the steamer, his brother was pleased to see him. Stripping the wallpaper with a wet sponge and a putty knife was slow going, although Brandon had actually made a lot of progress loosening the paper.

The work went much faster, however, with the help of the steamer. The room, which had already smelled musty, was soon filled with thick, stifling steam, but Jake worked hard, determined to finish as soon as possible.

Before long, the first strip of ancient wallpaper began to peel away from the wall next to the door. Like the wilting petal of some dying flower, it drooped, then fell slowly to the floor. Standing on top of the stepladder, Jake cheered, but the sound caught in his throat as he saw what was behind the paper.

Instead of bare and patchy plaster, part of a fabulous painting had been revealed. Its colors were surprisingly vivid, and it was the very last thing Jake had been expecting to see in the drab, musty old room. The painting appeared to depict a group of bearded men in fancy but old-fashioned clothes. They wore heavy black outfits with white ruffled collars and stood beside horses in a lush green field. Behind them, rolling hills stretched away toward the horizon under a cloudless, deep blue sky.

Brandon, who had just opened one of the windows to let out the worst of the steam, turned back at the sound of Jake's stifled cheer. He stood motionless, staring at the painting in amazement as Jake climbed slowly down the stepladder to join him. They both gazed silently for a moment at what they had uncovered.

Then Jake stepped forward, fascinated by the picture that lay behind the paper. "It's a mural, not a framed picture," he remarked, touching the tableau gently. "It's actually painted on the wall itself."

"Can you tell what time period it's supposed to be?" Brandon asked, his eyes never leaving the wall.

Jake shrugged. "I don't know," he said thoughtfully. "They're wearing *really* old-fashioned clothes. They look a lot like Pilgrims. Mom did say that this house is pretty old."

"Yeah, but it couldn't possibly be *that* old," Brandon said. "The colors are really bright. I'd have thought that after four hundred years they would have faded more than this."

"Maybe it's because the picture's been covered by this thick wallpaper for a while," Jake suggested. "Or maybe the painting's not as old as the house is. Maybe the wall was painted only fifty or sixty years ago. That might be why the colors are still so vivid."

Brandon nodded. "He doesn't look too happy, does he?" he commented, pointing toward a figure in the foreground.

It was a boy who appeared to be roughly the same age as Jake and Brandon. He was dressed like the men in the picture. However, unlike the men, who were looking at their horses, his painted face was staring out of the picture — right at the twins. The boy's expression was one of complete fear and disbelief.

Jake was studying the boy curiously when Brandon interrupted his thoughts.

"I wonder what that means," Brandon said, pointing to a gold border that ran along the top of the mural. It bore a phrase that appeared to be written in a foreign language.

"'*Fatum tuum, nisi celata fuerit pictura, idem erit,*'" Jake read aloud.

"It isn't French or Spanish," Brandon went on. "I don't recognize the words from anything we've done in school."

"Maybe it's Latin," Jake mused. "I mean, if the painting was created a long time ago, then that would make sense. Latin used to be more common than it is today, right?"

"I think so," Brandon replied. "I wonder if there's more of the mural on the rest of the wall." He started pulling at another piece of damp wallpaper.

Jake ran the steamer over this next section, and the boys removed the strip of wallpaper.

"Wow!" said Brandon with a gasp.

The blue sky featured in the first part of the mural remained the same, as did the bright green landscape forming the backdrop. Although only a small group of men appeared in the first section, the next part showed hundreds of them.

"It's a battle scene," Jake said in fascination, looking at the clusters of soldiers on foot and on horseback. "But these guys look different." He was intrigued by the fact that the opposing forces were dressed differently from each other. One side in the battle wore red uniforms and stood in a line carrying long muskets. Their opposition wore less fancy uniforms, but some of them, particularly the cavalry, looked like George Washington.

"It looks like something from the Revolutionary War," Brandon noted.

"So the first section is set around the time of the Pilgrims," Jake added, racking his brains to try and remember when the Revolutionary War had been. "But the Revolutionary War was later, wasn't it?"

"Yeah," Brandon confirmed. "The late seventeen hundreds."

"So this second section is showing something that happened nearly two centuries after the first section," Jake remarked. He looked up. "And there's more Latin writing over the top of it, too."

"I wonder if the same artist did it all," Brandon said thoughtfully.

"Maybe," Jake replied. "Maybe a modern artist did the whole thing."

"Which side do you think she was on?" Brandon wanted to know. He was looking at the figure of a girl, in the foreground of the latest section of the painting.

Jake stared at her curiously. It was hard to tell which side she was on because she didn't seem interested in the battle at all. Like the boy in the first part of the mural, she was the only one who seemed to be looking out of the painting, and, like the boy, there was an expression of fear on her face.

Eagerly, Jake and Brandon stripped more of the paper from the walls and found that the battle scene stretched another foot or so across the mural.

"The colors are still bright," Brandon remarked. "Just like in the first section."

Jake nodded. "I wonder if Grandaunt Lucy knows that this mural's here," he mused. "If the paper was put up fifty-odd years ago, she'd only have been a little girl at the time."

"Why don't you go and ask her?" Brandon suggested.

"And while you're down there, ask her if we can have a drink, too. All this work has made me thirsty."

"I'm not going," Jake protested, not especially eager to talk to his grandaunt.

"One of us has got to. Let's do rock-paper-scissors to decide," Brandon said.

Jake nodded and hid one hand behind his back.

"Ready," said Brandon. "One, two, three . . ."

Jake whipped his hand into view and groaned as Brandon did the same. Jake had chosen paper. Brandon had chosen scissors.

"I win!" Brandon grinned. "Scissors cut paper."

"Best of three?" Jake suggested hopefully, but the look on Brandon's face said it all. Jake headed out of the room as his brother turned back to uncover more of the mural.

Brandon ran the steamer over the next section of wallpaper, which was showing no sign of coming loose. He sighed and reached for his putty knife. He slid it underneath the edge of the paper, prying it carefully away from the wall.

Gradually, the strip came free and Brandon pulled it down, exposing a little more of the mural. Another strip soon followed as Brandon worked to uncover another section of the painting. He stepped back to look at the latest portion.

Once again, the clothes of the figures had changed. There was a small group of people who stood together on the bright green hillside. The women wore fancy dresses with tight corsets that reminded Brandon of his mom's favorite movie, *Gone with the Wind*.

"The Civil War era," murmured Brandon, recognizing additional details from pictures he'd seen at school. Again, the mural seemed to depict a scene more recent than the last one.

He felt something warm on his fingers and guessed it was some wallpaper glue. He frowned when he looked down to see that it was blood. Quickly he glanced at the blade of the putty knife and saw that there were two tiny specks of blood on that, too.

Had he cut himself? Brandon didn't see how that was possible; the blade was too blunt. It barely cut through the paper. He wiped the blood on his jeans and examined his hands. Then he shook his head in bewilderment: He had no cuts on his fingers.

Brandon shrugged. He looked back at the mural again — and what he saw made him feel as if his entire body had been dipped in ice water.

There was a figure in the foreground — just as there had been in all the other sections of the mural. And, just as in those other sections, this figure was looking directly out of the painting. It was a boy of about thirteen, dressed like Tom Sawyer or Huckleberry Finn. Both his hands were raised above his head as if he was surrendering, and the palm of his right hand bore a small, deep cut. Brandon could see a wet red splotch.

He touched it with the tip of his index finger, and it felt warm. He shivered uneasily. *The steamer must have caused the paint on the mural to run*, he told himself firmly. Yes, that had to be the answer.

He was still standing looking at the mural when the door of the room opened. Jake came in carrying two glasses of orange juice.

"I got our drinks," Jake said triumphantly, handing a glass to his brother.

Brandon took a sip of his orange juice, but continued to gaze at the boy in the mural with the injured palm. He glanced down again at the blade of the putty knife.

"Grandaunt Lucy said we can help ourselves to orange juice from the fridge," Jake went on. "She's not that bad really, you know."

Brandon nodded blankly, still completely distracted by the mural.

"Are you all right?" Jake asked, putting a hand on his brother's arm.

"I uncovered another piece of the mural," Brandon told him. "It's from the Civil War."

"Yeah, great," Jake said, reaching for something in his back pocket. "But look what I found while I was downstairs."

"I wonder who they are," Brandon said, gazing at the girls in the small black-and-white framed photograph that his brother held out.

"I saw the picture in the kitchen when I was getting our drinks," Jake said. "Don't you recognize them?" He jabbed a finger at the girls in the picture. They were about ten years old, wearing dresses with their hair in long pigtails. "Look at her face." Jake pointed to the girl on the right of the picture. "I think it's Grandaunt Lucy with her twin sister — the one who went missing. There are more pictures of them both downstairs."

"What's wrong with you? You'd better put it back, Jake," Brandon said anxiously. "If Grandaunt Lucy notices this is missing, we might end up with another punishment!"

"Chill out. I'll do it later," Jake said, stuffing the picture back into his jeans pocket. "She won't notice, anyway. She's outside in the garden."

"What was that noise?" Brandon asked, suddenly spinning around.

"I didn't hear anything," Jake replied, frowning.

"Listen," Brandon told him.

Jake stood still in the steamy room, straining his ears for the slightest sound. After a moment, he heard it: a slight rustling sound, not loud enough to be footsteps. It reminded Jake more of fingertips sliding across paper.

"Look," Brandon snapped, pointing toward the far wall of the room. "It's moving," he said. "The paper's moving!"

"There must be air bubbles trapped underneath it," Jake suggested, watching as the paper undulated gently.

Then, one by one, four small bulges began to appear in the paper, close to one another. To Brandon they looked like fingertips. It was almost as if someone was pressing against the wallpaper from the other side. "Air bubbles," Brandon repeated in an effort to reassure himself more than Jake.

"Come on," Jake insisted, reaching for the steamer. "Let's get the rest of the paper off the walls. I want to see what else is on this mural."

Time had lost all meaning for Brandon. He was only interested in tearing down the wallpaper and uncovering the rest of the mural. He knew that he and Jake had been working for several hours, but he didn't care.

"Can't we pack up for today?" Jake asked. "I'm sure Grandaunt Lucy won't mind if we come back and finish up tomorrow."

Brandon ignored him. In fact, he hardly heard

him. He was too immersed in stripping away more of the paper.

"Brandon, I said, let's leave it until tomorrow, OK? I'm worn out."

Brandon ignored his brother again. He didn't want to stop, and he was hoping that Jake would just give up.

"Brandon." Jake groaned insistently.

Brandon sighed. Clearly, he was going to have to answer. "I'm not leaving yet," he snapped.

Jake sighed but did not protest. However, while Jake stopped for a rest every now and then, Brandon kept using the steamer and his putty knife to tear off strips of the old paper. He gazed in awe at each freshly exposed section of the mural. In every case, the colors of the painting looked as bright and true-to-life as a digital photo.

By now, there was no question that the times depicted in the mural were changing, becoming closer to the present day. As Brandon tore another strip away, he discovered a section containing several figures that would not have looked out of place about a hundred years ago.

Brandon stepped back from the wall to the center of the room and looked around at what had been uncovered so far. Three walls had now been stripped to reveal the secrets beneath. Closest to the door was the Pilgrim scene. Then, moving clockwise, the other tableaux followed. The style of each was remarkably similar.

"Well, I think we can safely say that each scene wasn't painted during the period it shows," Brandon said thoughtfully.

"Why do you say that?" asked Jake.

"The style's the same in every section. So is the background," Brandon pointed out. "That means it was probably all done by one artist."

Jake nodded. "And there's one of those frightened figures looking out of the painting in every different historical period," he said.

"It would have taken one artist ages to paint all this," Brandon murmured.

"Not *hundreds of years* though." Jake grinned. "But, look, that Latin sentence is repeated above each section," he added. "I'd love to know what it means."

"Yeah, but we don't know anybody who speaks *Latin*," Brandon pointed out. "There's no way we can find out what it means."

Jake's eyes lit up. "Yes, there is," he said, smiling. "I could type it into a translation site on the Internet."

"And how are you going to do that? I don't think Grandaunt Lucy owns a computer," Brandon replied.

"Well, let's take a break, go home, and do it there," Jake suggested. "It won't take long."

"You go," Brandon told him, strangely unwilling to leave the mural. "I'll keep going here."

Jake gave him an odd look. "Are you sure? Why don't you come with me? Grandaunt Lucy won't mind."

"I said I'll keep working!" Brandon snapped. He saw a look of concern cross Jake's face and realized he'd been a bit short-tempered. "I'm sorry, it's just that, well, the sooner we get this job finished, the better, right?"

"OK," Jake agreed. "I'll run home, check out what those words mean, and come back."

Brandon was already attacking the remaining wallpaper with the steamer again. He nodded. "And put that picture back on your way out," he said, gesturing to the small framed photo sticking out of Jake's pocket. Then he turned back to the mural, anxious to see the next section.

"I won't be long," Jake said.

Brandon didn't answer him. He was too busy working. The door swung smoothly shut behind Jake with its customary little sigh, but Brandon barely heard it.

Now that he was alone in the room, Brandon's work reached a fever pitch. He steamed and scraped determinedly at the wallpaper, tearing it off, and hurling it away until only half of the fourth and final wall remained covered.

Breathing hard, he worked on, inspired by the knowledge that he had nearly finished. Soon he would be able to see the mural in its entirety. He eagerly tore away two more strips of wallpaper and staggered backward to see what he had revealed.

It was a group of men dressed in suits and neckties like the characters in black-and-white TV sitcoms. And in the foreground, there was another figure that seemed curiously out of place — not because of his clothes, but because of his attitude. This time it was a young boy, his hands to his head, his face contorted in a scream.

Brandon scanned the rest of the mural, his gaze traveling slowly through the historical progression from scene to scene. He was fascinated by the figures who stared out of the painting. He had the strong feeling that they were trying to tell him something. His gaze drifted up to the Latin phrase that was constantly repeated above the picture. Was *that* what the figures were trying to tell him? He wondered how long Jake had been gone. Would his brother manage to translate the Latin?

He was so impatient to know what the Latin meant that he reached for his cell phone. He intended to call Jake and see what he had learned, but then he saw that there were only three more strips of wallpaper left. Once those were removed, the entire mural would be visible. Perhaps then he would know what the strange frightened figures were trying to say. All thoughts of calling Jake were instantly forgotten.

Brandon picked up the steamer and the putty knife. He was determined to remove the last vestiges of the wallpaper. His breathing was shallow, his T-shirt soaked with sweat. When he tore away two of the final strips, he took a step back to see what he had uncovered.

He found himself looking at a scene from the 1960s. At least, he guessed it was the 1960s from the look of the bell-bottom pants worn by some of the figures. As he had come to expect, the transition from the previous scene to this one was seamless. The sky was still clear blue, the grass emerald green. And, apart from the figures that populated the background of the scene, there was one other figure who stared out of the mural with an expression so intense and lifelike that Brandon felt she was looking directly at him.

It was a pretty young girl with her blonde hair in pigtails. And as Brandon looked at her, in spite of the heat in the room, he felt icy cold. He tried to swallow, but it felt as if someone had filled his throat with chalk.

He knew that face. He had seen the girl's features before. He felt his heart pounding against his ribs as he rushed from the room and down the stairs. He found the photograph that he was looking for in the hallway and raced back upstairs to the mural, clutching his prize.

He held the small, framed picture of the two girls in pigtails up against the painting. And now there could be no doubt. The resemblance was just too strong. Even the clothes were the same. The little girl in the painting was identical to the one in the photograph. It was Grandaunt Lucy's missing sister.

Brandon almost dropped the photo. He looked from the picture in his hand to the painted figure on the wall and back again, but the likeness was unmistakable. He put down the photo and glanced at the last remaining strip of wallpaper.

He had to get that off. Had to see what lay beneath. His curiosity gnawed at him furiously, driving him on relentlessly as he ran the steamer over the last strip.

The last piece of wallpaper clung defiantly to the mural but, eventually, Brandon pulled the thick, crusty paper free. He hurled it to the floor and gazed at the final piece of the picture.

The mural showed a near-perfect representation of

Grandaunt Lucy's house, complete with the green hills that surrounded it and the dazzling blue sky above. And Brandon immediately recognized the inscription because the same words appeared in the other sections: *Fatum tuum, nisi celata fuerit pictura, idem erit.*

However, unlike the other parts of the mural, this last section contained no figures in the painted scene. Brandon frowned and moved closer, stretching out his fingertips.

In the foreground, there was an unpainted area. He could see bare wall where grass should have been. And as he peered at it, he felt the hairs on the back of his neck rise once more. The weird feeling that someone was blowing softly on the back of his neck struck Brandon again. He whirled around to see if Jake had returned, but there was no one there. He was alone in the room.

Suddenly, to his left, he heard a low groaning sound. He turned back to the mural, and what he saw almost caused him to scream in terror. The figure of Grandaunt Lucy's sister was moving toward him through the picture!

The painted figure grew larger as she drew nearer to the foreground of the mural. Her arms reached out toward Brandon, as if she was begging for help.

No! This is impossible, Brandon thought, but he couldn't tear himself away. The girl was now life-size, only slightly shorter than he was. Brandon was sure he could make out the lines and texture of her skin, as if her hand had actually come out *through the wall*.

Brandon shook his head and blinked, convinced that his eyes and his mind must be playing tricks on him. His heart pounding, he took a step closer to the mural.

As he approached, the girl reached out farther toward him, still with a pleading look on her face. In response, Brandon found himself slowly stretching out his own hand, until his fingertips touched hers.

Immediately, her hand shot forward into the room, her fingers grasping at Brandon's arm. This time, as her fingers closed around his wrist, Brandon *did* shout out in shock and fear. Instinctively, he tried to pull his arm away, but the girl's grip was uncannily strong and he could not free himself.

He looked up from the fingers around his arm into the eyes of the girl who held him. The expression on her face had changed now. It was filled with ugly and furious determination.

This isn't happening, Brandon thought frantically. *It's some kind of bizarre illusion, caused by heat, or too much work, or* something!

Wasn't it?

Suddenly, the hand tugged at him, hard, pulling him toward the mural. Brandon braced himself for the collision with the wall, but it never came. Instead, he felt a terrible sucking sensation all around him, as if the wall itself was swallowing him whole.

Brandon opened his mouth to scream, but the breath was knocked from his body as he landed heavily on what felt like grass. He lay on his back for a moment, trying to catch his breath. The familiar smell of fresh-cut grass filled his nostrils, and, above him, the sky was clear and blue.

Brandon struggled to his feet, his legs shaking a little, his mind still reeling from what had just happened. He quickly realized that he was standing in his grandaunt's front garden. The sun shined down upon him, and he could even feel a cool breeze against his skin.

In a daze, Brandon walked up to the front door and knocked hard — but his fist made no sound on the wood. And there was no answer from inside. He moved along to the nearest window, cupped his hands around his eyes, and peered through the murky glass. There was nothing inside. No dusty living room with crumbling plaster and hundreds of portraits. Just a wall of darkness — as if somebody had painted the glass itself black.

Brandon looked to his right and left, becoming more terrified by the second. Beyond the house and its gardens, green fields stretched away.

"Brandon!" came Jake's voice suddenly.

As Brandon turned, his jaw dropped. Where the blue sky met the horizon, he could see the room in Grandaunt Lucy's house that he had just left. The realization hit him like a thunderbolt: He was *inside* the painting!

Jake was coming through the door.

"Jake, over here!" Brandon yelled desperately. "I'm inside the painting! Help me!" But Brandon could see that Jake wasn't hearing a word he said.

"Brandon, the Latin words," Jake called. "They mean 'your fate will be the same if the mural is not concealed.'"

Trapped within the mural, looking out at his brother, Brandon knew how true those words actually were. He shouted Jake's name until he was hoarse, but his brother only stared blankly around the room.

"'Your fate will be the same if the mural is not concealed,'" Jake mumbled again, then headed toward the door. He was about to leave when Grandaunt Lucy entered, carrying several rolls of fresh, new wallpaper and a big tub of paste.

"I brought this new wallpaper for you to put up," she said brightly, stepping into the room. "What's this?" she asked, pausing as she saw the spectacular mural that now stretched around all four walls of the bedroom.

Brandon watched her gaze finally settle on a section of the painting that seemed to be to his right.

She let the rolls of wallpaper and the paste fall from

her arms. "My sister!" she exclaimed softly, her voice cracking. She took a step toward the wall. "That's my sister, Josephine!" she screamed, and she began clawing at the wall as if trying to reach into the mural. "Josie!"

Brandon wondered if perhaps Grandaunt Lucy would be able to hear him. "Get me out, please!" he shrieked, watching his grandaunt scrabbling at the wall. "Help me!"

But neither Grandaunt Lucy nor Jake seemed able to hear him at all.

Brandon saw Jake trying to pull his grandaunt away from the wall.

"Why can't you see me?" Brandon screamed from inside the mural. "Jake, help!"

But Jake was more concerned with helping Grandaunt Lucy. "No, no. It's just a picture. Just try to relax and calm down," he said gently. "Why don't you lie down? I'll start putting up the new wallpaper."

Grandaunt Lucy wiped her eyes with a little lace handkerchief and nodded. "Thank you," she whimpered. "But the girl in the painting, she looks just like my twin sister."

"I know," Jake told her. "But it's just a picture."

Brandon raised his hands in desperation. *It's not just a picture*, he thought. "Jake, look at me!" he tried shouting again, his throat now sore with the effort. "Help me!"

Grandaunt Lucy moved slowly out of the room, and Jake pried the lid off the tub of wallpaper paste. Then, as Brandon watched, he moved the stepladder into position and reached for a roll of the new wallpaper. Carefully, he laid it out on the floor and covered it with paste. Holding it up in front of him, Jake walked toward the mural where Brandon was imprisoned and climbed the stepladder.

"Jake, help me. Please, help me. Get me out of here. *Please!*" Brandon screamed, now sobbing with fear and desperation.

But Jake merely lifted the piece of wallpaper and prepared to smooth it into place on the wall.

"No," pleaded Brandon from inside the mural. "NOOOO!"

TRUE COLORS

The words buzzed like angry bees in her ears. Carrie Peterson leaned forward in the passenger seat of the car and eased the volume of the CD player up a notch, trying to drive away the words.

Her mother hadn't stopped talking since they'd left the house that morning. Or, at least, that's how it felt to Carrie. Not that this morning was any different from all the others. Every day, it was the same earache.

"You did do your homework, didn't you, Carrie?" Mrs. Peterson asked.

"Yes, Mom," Carrie said, trying to concentrate on the music and tune out her mom as much as possible.

"And you did sign up for drama class after school, didn't you?" her mother continued.

"Yes, Mom," answered Carrie, somehow keeping her fixed smile in place.

"Did you comb your hair this morning?" Mrs. Peterson asked doubtfully, glancing at her.

"Yes, Mom."

"It doesn't look like it."

"It's supposed to look like this, Mom," Carrie said, pulling down the sun visor on her side of the car. She inspected her image in the mirror, stroking a hand through her hair. Her natural color was strawberry blonde, but she'd recently added some pink highlights.

"I hope that dye washes out," Mrs. Peterson said, smoothing her own immaculately cut and styled blonde hair.

"It'll wash out after three days, Mom," Carrie explained patiently. "Just like the last one."

"You mean the sky-blue one? The one your principal threatened to give you a week's detention for?" Mrs. Peterson asked.

Carrie nodded. "Mrs. Collins hasn't got a clue about how to dress. I wouldn't expect her to appreciate my hair or my fashion sense. Why is everyone so bothered by the way I look, anyway?" she went on, feeling mutinous. "It's no one's business except mine. Just because most people don't get it, doesn't mean there's anything wrong with it. It's my style — just like yours is all about designer labels."

"At least my clothes don't have holes in them. I'd look a little ridiculous showing up for work dressed the way you are, wouldn't I?" Mrs. Peterson pointed out.

Carrie glanced down at the outfit she'd so thoughtfully assembled for herself that day. She wore a bright green long-sleeved T-shirt, complete with a grinning face on the front, as well as a red cardigan decorated with buttons featuring her favorite bands. Her flared jeans were faded and threadbare on both knees, and her striped socks were visible above her sneakers. "Didn't you ever experiment with fashion when you were my age?" Carrie asked with a sigh.

"Of course, I did," her mother replied. "But that didn't include dyeing my hair so that it looked as if someone had put cotton candy on my head!"

"Well, my real friends think that my style is cool, and I like it. That's all that matters," Carrie said firmly.

Her mom sighed and brought the car to a halt near the schoolyard. Carrie reached into the backseat and dragged her latest pride and joy onto her lap. It was a large customized retro canvas bag.

"Have you got your gym bag?" her mother asked as Carrie clambered out of the car.

Carrie smiled and dangled the bag in front of her mom.

"I doubt any of the other girls have a bag like that," Mrs. Peterson remarked.

"That's the whole point, Mom," Carrie said, sighing. She slammed the car door behind her and heard the electric window whir as it was lowered.

"Have a good day," her mom called. "Try not to annoy too many people." She gave Carrie a wink to let her know she was half joking.

"I'll do my best, Mom." Carrie forced herself to smile. "Are you working late again this evening?"

"It's difficult to say," her mother replied. "I'll do my best to be home by six, but you know it's not easy. See you later."

Carrie nodded, watching her mom drive away. "No, Mom," she murmured wearily. "It's never easy, is it?"

Well, I think it's great," said Chloe Walker. "I wish I had a bag like it."

Carrie smiled as her friend Chloe got a closer look at the retro bag. It was lunch break, and the girls' first chance to catch up. Carrie stepped nimbly out of the way as a younger boy ran past, quickly followed by a bunch of his friends.

"Did you do all those designs yourself?" Chloe asked, turning the bag over.

Carrie nodded. "And I sewed the patches on," she said. "My mom hates it . . . obviously. But she hates everything about my style."

"All parents hate what we wear, do, say, and listen to." Chloe grinned. "It's their job."

The two girls laughed, but they were abruptly interrupted by another voice.

"Who sold you that bag, Carrie?"

Carrie rolled her eyes and turned in the direction of the voice.

"They should get charged with a crime!" Lisa Jameson continued, smiling brightly. Behind her, the five girls who always followed Lisa around giggled nastily.

"Or maybe you found it in the Dumpster behind school?" Lisa went on. There was more laughter.

"Can't your mom give you shopping advice?" Lisa demanded. "She's a pretty stylish woman. She must be embarrassed, letting you come to school with something like that." Lisa peered disdainfully at the bag. "You should get her to buy you something decent."

"I like this bag, thanks," Carrie responded. "Everyone has their own personal taste, you know."

"Yes, I know, and yours is *terrible*," Lisa replied. The girls around her laughed.

"Well, I'm not going to argue with you, Lisa," Carrie said wearily, raising her voice so she could be heard over the chorus of laughter. She turned to walk away. "Come on, Chloe."

"Go ahead," Lisa called. "Run away. Maybe you'll find a nice sweater or a pair of pants lying in a mud puddle."

Carrie felt her cheeks burn as she and Chloe walked off, the other girls' laughter ringing in their ears.

"I hate her," Chloe said as they made their way from the playground toward the girls' room.

Carrie didn't speak. For a moment, she thought she was going to cry, but that feeling quickly turned into anger. In the restroom, Carrie approached one of the sinks and studied her reflection in the mirror. She turned the faucet and began washing her hands.

"Lisa's frightened of being different," Carrie said angrily. "She wants to be like everyone else. She wants to look like them, talk like them, and act like them. Those girls that hang around with her are just like sheep. They're all pathetic."

Chloe nodded in agreement.

"First Mom and now Lisa Jameson," Carrie said with a groan, drying her hands. "Maybe my mom switched babies when I was born. She likes designer stuff, and so does Lisa. My mom's got blonde hair, and so does Lisa."

"Well, you have *natural* blonde hair," Chloe pointed out. "It's just that you dye yours a different color every month."

"Well, you know what they say: Variety is the spice of life! Next month, I think I'll go for bright red." Carrie laughed. "Or maybe neon green. That'll really get everyone going."

Both girls chuckled, the sound filling the restroom. Carrie looked at her reflection in the mirror one more time and felt her mood lift. It would take more than Lisa Jameson and her idiotic followers to bother her. She ran a hand through her hair and grinned at her mirror image.

When the bell rang at the end of the school day, Carrie marched outside with her fellow pupils, who scattered in different directions as they headed home. Carrie soon found herself alone in the schoolyard. As she paused to heave her bag onto her shoulder, someone stepped out in front of her. Carrie felt her heart sink.

"Like the cardigan, Carrie," Lisa Jameson said with a giggle. "*Not.*"

The girls around Lisa laughed as they gazed at Carrie's red cardigan with its carefully placed buttons.

Carrie opened her mouth to say something, then decided against it. She stepped around Lisa and began walking home.

"It's the same color as my dog's blanket!" one of the girls called after her.

"Perhaps it *is* your dog's blanket," one of the others added to more laughter. "It looks like it."

Just ignore them, Carrie told herself. *They're not worth your time.*

Carrie kept walking, but the girls followed behind her and they wouldn't shut up.

Lisa stepped up to Carrie, a look of triumph on her face. "You're just too emotional, Carrie." She smirked. "That's your problem."

Carrie stood still on the sidewalk as Lisa and the other girls ran off down the street, one of them turning to wave mockingly at Carrie.

"Idiots," Carrie said under her breath, reaching for her cell phone as she felt it vibrate. She pulled it from her jacket pocket and saw that she had a text message. It was from her mom.

Running late.
Could you and Mark handle dinner?
Love, Mom

Carrie sighed and dropped the cell phone back into her pocket. "Thanks, Mom," she murmured. *This is turning into a really bad day*, she thought, her earlier good mood forgotten.

Hey, Carrie!"

"Amy!" Carrie beamed at the sight of her cousin running toward her. "What are you doing here?"

"I thought I'd check out the farmer's market in the park on my way home from school," Amy replied.

Carrie's smile broadened. "I'll come with you." She and Amy had been friends all their lives, even though they now went to different schools. The girls walked through the iron gates of the park. "But I can't stay out too late," she said.

"Why not?" asked Amy.

"Mom's working late again." Carrie sighed. "Mark and I have to get dinner ready for when Dad gets home."

"I saw a fire engine this morning, and your dad was driving it," Amy said. "He waved to me as he went past."

"I hope he wasn't called to a big fire," Carrie said anxiously. "I always worry about him when he's working."

The two girls walked on in silence for a moment. Then the farmer's market came into view. It was a symphony of colors, smells, sights, and sounds. The colored awnings seemed to create a rainbow effect in Carrie's eyes. Most of the vendors offered fresh fruits and vegetables, but there were always other surprises, too.

The girls reached the first of the stalls and stopped to look at the handmade jewelry that had been carefully laid out on a black velvet cloth.

Amy picked up a silver daisy brooch with a tiger's eye in the center. She held it against Carrie's cardigan. "It looks good on you," she said.

Carrie smiled but shook her head when she saw the price. "Yeah, but I can't afford fifty dollars," she replied.

Amy put back the brooch, and the two girls moved on, past more stalls selling everything from hand-drawn charcoal sketches to scented candles.

"Let's take a look over there," Carrie said, nodding toward a stall displaying various books and magazines. "I need something new to read."

Most of the hardcovers on display were discolored with age, and many no longer had their dust jackets.

Amy inspected the spines to check the titles, while Carrie picked up a book and leafed through the yellowed pages.

"Look at the cover of this one!" Amy exclaimed, pointing out a book about astronomy. It showed a silver-painted telescope surrounded by fading stars that made up the name of the book's author.

Carrie smiled, but she was more interested in the old magazines that were laid out at one end of the stall. "Some of these magazines are more than thirty years old," she said, picking up a copy of *Film Review*. "They're practically antiques!"

"Five dollars each, sweetheart," said the old woman who ran the stall. "Take your time deciding."

She smiled thinly at Carrie, pulling her coat more tightly around herself. Her hair was long and gray, held in a ponytail by a wide, black velvet band. She had thin, pinched features and the bluest eyes Carrie had ever seen.

"Are you going to buy anything?" Amy asked.

Carrie didn't answer. She wasn't looking at the magazines, but at the right arm of the old woman running the stall. She had her hand shoved firmly into the money belt she wore around her waist and, Carrie noted, she never removed it, not even to serve her customers.

"What are you getting, Carrie?" Amy persisted.

Carrie tore her gaze away from the old woman and scanned the covers of the magazines. One of them suddenly caught her eye. "Look at this," she said, picking it up. "I've got to get this. Look at the date on it. It's the same as my birthday."

"It comes with a free gift, too," Amy noticed. "Look — stuck to the cover."

"Can I take this one, please?" Carrie asked the old lady, handing the magazine over and digging in her purse for a five-dollar bill.

"Good choice, dear," the old lady said, putting the magazine down and extending her left hand to take the money. "It's very rare. It'll be worth much more than five dollars in a few years." She reached out to hand the magazine back to Carrie, but before doing so, the old lady deftly twisted the free gift away from the cover and dropped it into her coat pocket.

"Doesn't that come with the magazine?" Carrie asked, a little irritated at being denied her free gift.

The old lady merely shook her head.

"It was a mood ring, right?" Carrie said, pointing at the cover. "Look, it says here on the cover that there's a chart inside to tell you what the different colors mean when the ring changes. I've always wanted a mood ring."

"You wouldn't want that one, dear," the old lady said firmly.

"Can I have the ring that goes with the magazine, please?" Carrie persisted.

"The *magazine* was five dollars, dear," the old lady said coldly, glaring at Carrie with her icy blue eyes. "Not the ring." And, with that, she turned her back on Carrie and began putting the books and magazines from her stall into cardboard boxes.

"How much do you want for the ring?" Carrie demanded, feeling exasperated. "I really would like it."

"I don't mean to be rude," the woman said over her shoulder. "But it's time for me to pack up my stall. If you're desperate for a ring, visit Bob's stall on the other side of the market. His selection is absolutely lovely."

As the woman hastily shoved magazines into cardboard boxes, Carrie could see that her face was flushed. It was clear that the old woman wanted her to go, but a streak of stubbornness kept Carrie rooted to the spot. For some reason, she felt like she had to have that ring. "I'll give you twenty dollars for it," Carrie finally told the woman.

"The ring's not for sale, dear. I sell magazines, not rings."

Carrie and Amy looked quizzically at each other for a moment, then back at the old woman who had managed to clear her stall with amazing speed. The remaining books and magazines had been put away, and she had piled the boxes into a rusty shopping cart. The girls watched as the old lady hurried off, pushing the shopping cart in front of her.

"It was only a cheap old mood ring, Carrie," Amy said. "Come on, let's see what else we can find before the other stalls pack up."

Carrie nodded, and the two girls moved on through the market. They stopped at a stall selling hats and tried on a few. They bought chocolate chip cookies at another stall and ate them hungrily. Then, just as Carrie was thinking about heading home, Amy spotted a heart-shaped pendant that she couldn't resist. She bought it and hung it around her neck.

"It looks great," Carrie told her, admiring it. "Do you want to get anything else?"

"No, thanks," Amy replied. "It's getting cold now. I think I'd better go home."

"Good idea," Carrie agreed, and the girls turned toward the gates.

As they were leaving, something shiny caught Carrie's eye. A small metal object was lying in the grass, close to the old woman's magazine stall, which was now empty.

Carrie hurried across and bent down to retrieve the item. "It's the mood ring!" she exclaimed in surprise. "It must have fallen out of the old lady's pocket when she was packing up her stuff."

"Are you going to keep it?" Amy asked.

"Well, I bought the magazine," Carrie pointed out. "And the ring was attached to it."

Amy nodded. "Yeah, and it was supposed to be a free gift."

Carrie looked at the ring thoughtfully for a moment, then dropped it into her pocket.

"That lady probably doesn't even realize it's missing," Amy said. "And now I really have to get home. My mom will be wondering where I am."

"Me, too," Carrie agreed. "I can't let Mark make dinner on his own. He'll kill me."

Amy laughed and waved and the girls hurried off in opposite directions.

Carrie grinned to herself. For the first time that day, she felt really happy.

The house was warm when Carrie got home, and the delicious aroma of cooking wafted through from the kitchen.

"It's me!" she called, kicking off her shoes.

"About time," her brother answered from the kitchen. "I've already started dinner."

Carrie felt in her pocket for the mood ring. Her fingers closed around it, and she withdrew it eagerly, turning it over and over in the palm of her hand. It glistened darkly in the light. Slowly, she pushed it onto her right index finger.

It was a perfect fit. Carrie smiled — something about it just felt right. It was almost as if it had been made for her. She looked down at the magazine cover. LOOK INSIDE TO SEE HOW TO USE YOUR MOOD RING it read.

"I'll come help in a minute, Mark," Carrie called distractedly, heading for the living room.

"Dad called and said he'll be home in about half an hour," her brother shouted back.

Carrie nodded and sat down on the sofa, flicking through the old magazine. DOES THE RING MATCH YOUR MOOD? proclaimed the lettering across the center pages. Carrie scanned the color chart:

COLOR	MOOD
LIGHT BLUE	Happy
PINK	Optimistic
DARK BLUE	Sad
RED	Angry
PURPLE	Afraid

BROWN	Confused
GREEN	Jealous
ORANGE	Content
YELLOW	Ill
GRAY	Tired

Curiously, Carrie checked the color of the ring against the color chart in the magazine. The stone was light blue. She nodded. *More than a perfect fit,* Carrie said to herself happily. *It's got my mood right, too.*

"Carrie, are you going to come and help me or what?" her brother yelled from the kitchen.

She glanced at the ring, wondering if it had changed color. No. Apparently, there wasn't a color for "irritated by older brother." She smiled to herself. "I'm coming!" she shouted.

Carrie had just gotten up again when the phone rang. "I'll get it," Carrie called, reaching for the receiver. "It's probably Mom to say she's on her way."

She picked up the phone. "Hello?" she said.

"Hello, is this Carrie?" said a slightly nasal voice at the other end of the line.

"Yes," Carrie replied.

"It's Caroline," said the caller. Caroline was her mom's personal assistant. "Your mom asked me to remind you to turn off the oven after you've finished making dinner."

"OK, thanks, Caroline," Carrie said wearily. "Did she say what time she'd be home?"

"No, sorry. She's in a meeting at the moment."

"So you don't know how long she's going to be?" Carrie asked.

"No, but it could be an hour or more. You know what these meetings are like."

"Yes, I know," Carrie said unhappily. "OK. Thanks for calling, Caroline. Bye." She put down the receiver and sighed heavily.

As she took her hand away from the phone, she glanced at the mood ring. The stone was still light blue, but even as she watched, it began to darken. Like day becoming night, the shade of blue changed until it was deep navy. Carrie didn't have to check the color chart to know what navy meant. It was the color of sadness. The ring seemed to be working perfectly.

Carrie headed for the kitchen.

"You took your time," said her brother as she walked in. "Who was that on the phone?"

"Caroline," Carrie told him. "But she didn't know what time Mom would be home."

"Great," Mark said with a sigh.

As he spoke, Carrie glanced around the kitchen. It looked as if a bomb had gone off. There were empty packages on the countertops and potato peelings on the floor by the sink. Although the kitchen table hadn't been set, milk had been spilled on it.

"Mark, anyone would think you were six, not sixteen!" Carrie snapped. "Look at the mess you've made!"

"I've been getting dinner ready," her brother explained, pointing to the casserole bubbling in the oven. "If you'd been here to help, you could have cleaned up."

"Why should I clean up *your* mess?" Carrie demanded.

"OK, OK, take it easy. Messy rooms don't usually bother you; I've seen your bedroom," Mark said with a laugh.

"Oh, very funny! Well, *you* made this mess so *you* clean it up — or else Dad won't be very happy when he comes home," Carrie replied, feeling surprisingly annoyed by Mark's attempt at humor.

"At least give me a hand."

"Forget it!"

"Thanks." Mark sighed irritably. "You weren't here to help cook, you could at least help clean up."

"Don't tell me what to do!" Carrie yelled, completely losing her temper. "I'm sick of you trying to boss me around just because you're older!"

Mark didn't say anything. Carrie could see him eyeing her warily, and this really bugged her.

"And don't look at me like that," she went on. "Just because I won't clean up your mess doesn't mean there's anything wrong with me. You're just selfish, and I'm not putting up with it anymore!" Carrie suddenly realized that she was trembling all over.

"All right, all right," Mark said soothingly, sounding genuinely worried. "I'm sorry I made such a mess. It's never upset you like this before."

Realizing that was true, Carrie raised her hands in a gesture of surrender. As she did, she noticed that the mood ring was now glowing bright red: the color of anger. She glared at her brother, but kept her mouth tightly closed for fear of what she might say next. She still felt angry, but she also had a strong feeling that she might have been a little unfair. She took some deep breaths and felt the anger slowly start to subside.

"I'll help you straighten up," Carrie said quietly, once she could trust herself to speak.

Mark nodded, watching her closely, clearly uncertain how she was going to react next. Then he began wiping one of the counters.

Carrie stood motionless for a moment, unable to believe she had lost her temper with Mark like that. He was right, it wasn't like her. She tried to tell herself that it was just because she'd had a bad day, but something at the back of her mind told her that wasn't entirely true.

She shook her head in puzzlement and began to help her brother. As she reached out to pick up a box of gravy mix, she saw that the mood ring had changed color again. The angry red was now replaced by the brown of confusion.

Carrie nodded, agreeing with the ring. Then she heard the front door open.

"It's only me," called a tired voice.

Their dad wandered into the kitchen and sat down wearily on one of the chairs. He looked shattered. His eyes were red, and Carrie could see the dirt on his cheeks and hands.

"Are you all right, Dad?" she asked.

He shook his head. "There was a fire at a warehouse just outside town," he said grimly. "I've been there for hours. It took us all day to get it under control. Part of the roof collapsed and two people were injured. We just couldn't get them out in time."

Carrie and her brother drew close to their dad, seeing the exhaustion and distress on his face and wanting to be supportive.

"I think I'll go up to bed if you don't mind," he said, smiling at them. "I'm afraid I won't be very good company tonight. I'm pretty worn out. Sorry about the dinner."

Mark shook his head. "It's nothing, don't worry," he said. He and Carrie exchanged a glance, and Carrie felt a stab of guilt. Whatever had made her lose her temper paled into insignificance beside her dad's story.

Carrie gave her dad a hug before he went upstairs. She felt awful thinking about the terrible day her dad had faced, but she also felt a twinge of resentment. *Another great night at home with the family*, she thought. "I think I'll go to bed, too," she told her brother.

"Great," Mark groaned. "Am I supposed to eat dinner on my own?"

Carrie could only shrug as she turned and headed for the stairs. When she put her hand on the banister, she saw that the mood ring was now a dull gray. "Tired," Carrie said aloud, noticing the color. "Accurate, aren't you?"

The rain had been falling steadily ever since Carrie woke up that morning. Now, during her lunch break, she sat in the cafeteria watching the raindrops pelt the glass of the school windows. *I hate the rain*, she murmured to herself.

Her eyelids felt heavy with tiredness. Her sleep the previous night had been constantly interrupted by bad dreams.

Carrie rubbed her eyes. Because of the rain, no one had been allowed outside at lunchtime. She looked away from the window and glanced around the room. There was a constant babbling noise in the background as the other kids laughed and chatted.

Some magazines on a nearby table caught Carrie's eye, so she reached for one. As she did, she saw Lisa Jameson sauntering toward her, her usual little clique in tow.

"Nice ring. Which ninety-nine-cent store did you get it from, Carrie?" Lisa said with a sneer, and the other girls burst out laughing.

Carrie tried to ignore them. She fixed her gaze on the magazine.

"Which designer made it?" Lisa continued loudly. "Salvation Army?"

That provoked a second round of giggling.

"You'd better be careful that cheap metal doesn't turn your finger green," Lisa went on, reveling in the fact that she had an audience. "I bet your mom doesn't like it. Isn't it too cheap for her? Of course, I think you're a little too cheap for your mom altogether. That's probably why she never spends any time with you."

Carrie felt anger swelling up inside her, but she realized that it was mixed with something else. A feeling much stronger than rage. She stole a glance at her mood ring, expecting to see it glowing red to reflect her fury. She was a little surprised to see that it was bright green: the color of jealousy. *Why am I jealous of Lisa?* Carrie wondered.

"Then again, *no one* spends much time with you," Lisa murmured, wandering idly away from Carrie toward the other side of the room.

Carrie felt her patience snap. Before she knew what she was doing, she shot to her feet in fury and took a couple of steps toward Lisa. Carrie realized that Lisa was smiling now. It pleased Lisa to get a reaction from Carrie. That thought made Carrie stop.

"Maybe if you knew how to fit in, instead of trying to pretend you're such an individual, you'd have some friends," Lisa continued, clearly trying to provoke Carrie further. "That way, you wouldn't have to be jealous of people like me."

Is that why I'm jealous? Carrie wondered. *Do I really want friends like Lisa's?* She frowned and glanced down at the mood ring. It was still green for jealousy, glinting in the light like a cat's eye. Even though the ring appeared to confirm Lisa's snide remark, Carrie couldn't bear to think that Lisa was right.

"Maybe you should look at the things I wear, Carrie," Lisa was saying airily. "You might pick up some tips."

Carrie felt rage burn through her again. This time she whirled around and headed for the door. She wanted to be as far away from Lisa Jameson as possible. As she walked out of the room, she heard Lisa and her friends laughing again. The mood ring still shined green.

Carrie picked up the TV remote and jabbed one of the buttons.

"Is this what our evening's going to consist of?" Her dad chuckled. "Four hours of music videos and reality TV?"

"No, Dad," Carrie told him, pushing a piece of pizza into her mouth. "It's only *three* hours."

They both laughed and continued eating. Carrie felt happier than she had in ages. Her dad had been off-duty all day and just seeing him when she'd arrived home from school had lifted her spirits. When he'd told her that he had the rest of the night off and that they could order pizza, she hadn't needed to look at the mood ring to see its color; she knew it would be showing light blue — for happiness.

"Did Mom say what time she was coming home?" Carrie asked.

"No. She's having dinner with some people from work tonight so it'll probably be late."

"And Mark's at his friend's house, so that means we don't have to save *him* any pizza," Carrie added.

Her dad laughed and grabbed another slice. "I'd better get some of this for myself before you inhale the rest," he teased. "I don't know where you put it all. You must have hollow legs."

Carrie reached for another piece of pizza, but stopped suddenly when she felt her stomach ache as if it had been punched by a cold and invisible fist. She sat back in her chair, hoping that the feeling would subside.

"Are you OK, Carrie?" her dad asked, looking worried.

She nodded. "I just feel cold suddenly," she said, gazing blankly at the TV screen as she tried to figure out what was wrong. She could feel the hairs on the back of her neck standing up, and the chill that had struck her stomach was now seeping through her whole body. Carrie swallowed hard, not understanding why she felt so uncomfortable. And so *frightened*.

Her dad was still looking at her with concern when his cell phone rang. He hesitated a moment before picking it up. "Hello," he said. Carrie watched his face. "When?" he asked. "Whereabouts?"

Carrie saw his expression darken.

"How many are involved?" he demanded, listening intently. Then he nodded. "All right. Give me five minutes." He hung up the phone and got to his feet. "Are you going to be all right, Carrie? I'm afraid I've got to go," he said, already heading for the door. "There's a house fire on the other side of town. It's badly out of control and spreading."

"It's OK, Dad, I'll be fine," Carrie said a little sadly.

"At least now you get to finish all the pizza," he told her with a grin.

Carrie followed him to the front door and watched as he pulled on his coat and shoes and sprinted out to his car.

"Be careful, Dad," she called as he reversed out into the street, spun the wheel, and sped away. The car's taillights disappeared around the corner. Carrie closed the front door and headed back to the living room. She couldn't resist a glance at her mood ring. It was purple: the color of fear.

Carrie wasn't surprised. She got scared every time her dad was called to a big fire. The thought of him battling against the flames always made her nervous but, for some unknown reason, this time she felt even more uneasy than usual. Perhaps because she'd felt a surge of fear even before the phone rang. It was almost as if she had somehow known that bad news was coming. But Carrie knew that was crazy. It had been a coincidence and nothing more. Right?

Again she gazed at the ring and saw that it had changed color once more. It was now the muddy brown of confusion. Carrie smiled and shook her head, puzzled by how accurately the ring seemed to reflect her feelings. She looked at the remains of the pizza on the table, but she didn't feel like eating anymore. It was too early to go to bed, so she curled up on the sofa to watch TV.

The evening seemed to pass terribly slowly, but Carrie was determined to wait up until her dad got home. She had a cold feeling in the pit of her stomach. Something felt wrong. Something she couldn't put her finger on. A growing feeling of dread. Carrie knew she wouldn't be able to relax until her dad was back safe and sound, but the TV was failing to distract her from the worries tumbling through her mind. She reached for a magazine and thumbed through that instead, but the contents didn't register. Finally, she decided to see if some homework would occupy her thoughts. She opened her biology textbook, but the assigned chapter just didn't seem to make any sense. After reading one page twice, Carrie decided to give up and make herself a cup of tea.

She was barely off the sofa when the phone rang. She snatched it up. "Hello," she said nervously.

"Carrie, it's Dad," said the voice at the other end of the line.

Immediately, Carrie felt a wave of relief sweep through her. "I was worried about you, Dad," she told him, balancing the receiver in the crook of her neck so that she could hold her right hand up in front of her face. The mood ring shined with the bright, light blue of happiness.

"I'm fine, sweetheart," he told her. "Listen to me, Carrie, that fire I was called to, it was at the Jameson family's house. You go to school with their daughter, don't you?"

"Lisa, yes. Why?" Carrie replied.

There was a moment's silence at the other end of the line, then her dad started speaking again. He sounded grim. "The fire was out of control by the time the first fire engines arrived," he said. "They think a gas explosion started it, which is why it was so fierce. It began in the kitchen."

Carrie sat down as she listened, her heart beating hard against her ribs.

"Both of Lisa's parents are doing fine," her dad went on. "They were lucky. But Lisa . . . wasn't as lucky."

Carrie felt slightly sick as her father continued.

"She's in the hospital," he said softly. "And I know she's a friend of yours so I wanted to be the one to tell you."

Carrie didn't know what to say.

The auditorium at school was full the following morning. As Carrie entered slowly with the rest of her class, the subdued atmosphere revealed that news of the tragic fire had spread rapidly. On the stage at the front of the room, two teachers were speaking quietly, one of them dabbing at her eyes with a handkerchief. Even the youngest kids, sitting right at the front, were silent.

Carrie sat down next to Chloe.

"I feel so bad for her," Chloe said.

Carrie nodded. "I couldn't sleep last night," she said. "I know Lisa and I didn't get along, but I wouldn't have wished something like that on her." She rubbed her face with both hands and gazed at the stage as the principal stood up to speak.

"As you probably all know by now," Mrs. Collins began in her most somber tone, "there was a tragic event last night involving one of this school's students, Lisa Jameson, and her family."

Carrie heard some sniffling from her left-hand side and saw that Danielle Harrison, one of Lisa's friends, was crying softly.

"Lisa is a very popular girl," Mrs. Collins continued. "Thoughtful, caring, hardworking, and always ready to help others."

Carrie shook her head slightly at that. *Thoughtful and caring?* Not the Lisa she knew!

"Lisa is an exemplary member of the school community," Mrs. Collins went on. "The doctors are confident she'll make a full recovery, and I am, too. In fact, I think this minor setback will soon prove exactly how amazing Lisa Jameson truly is."

As Mrs. Collins collected her thoughts for a moment, Carrie could still hear sobs from the audience.

Mrs. Collins was far from finished. "Now, I'd like for us all to observe a moment of silence so that we may send our positive, healing thoughts her way."

Carrie bowed her head but, as she did, she noticed that the mood ring had turned light blue.

She blinked in disbelief. It was definitely light blue — indicating *happiness!* Carrie frowned. She didn't feel happy about what had happened to Lisa. They might not have been friends, but she hadn't wished Lisa any harm.

The auditorium remained silent — except that Carrie could still hear the muffled sounds of several people crying. At the same time, she felt the corners of her mouth lift in the beginnings of a smile. In horror, she realized that a broad, happy grin was spreading uncontrollably across her face. Carrie put her hand over her mouth, anxious that no one should see her, but the smile was growing.

Carrie couldn't understand what was happening to her. She bit the inside of her lip hard in an effort to stop the smile, but then, to her astonishment, she felt laughter bubbling up inside her, threatening to erupt into giggles.

Chloe glanced sideways at her, clearly wondering what was wrong, but Carrie could only meet her puzzled stare with a grin.

And then it happened: Carrie burst out laughing. The sound exploded from her, sounding horribly loud in the silence of the room. Chloe nudged her hard in the ribs. Others turned to stare at her — some in surprise, some in anger or confusion. And Carrie tried desperately to stop her laughter, but she couldn't.

"Shut up!" someone nearby hissed.

But Carrie was finding it impossible to stop laughing. She put both hands over her mouth to try and stifle the sound, but it was useless. She was laughing so hard that her belly was beginning to ache.

Out of the corner of her eye, she saw one of her teachers, Mr. Wainwright, heading angrily in her direction. Yet Carrie still couldn't stop herself. Big, heaving belly laughs continued to shake her, the sound reverberating around the auditorium.

Carrie felt a hand on her arm. Still laughing like a maniac, she was dragged out of her seat by Mr. Wainwright, who whispered something angrily in her ear about a lack of respect.

Heads turned in her direction as Carrie was virtually pushed from the auditorium through the double doors that led out to the playing field.

"I've never seen behavior like this!" snapped Mr.

Wainwright as soon as they were outside. "You should be ashamed of yourself!"

A blast of cold air hit Carrie once she was outside. It felt like a bucket of cold water had been poured over her head. Finally, Carrie managed to get the horrible laughter under control. She stood still, taking deep breaths.

Carrie could see that many of her classmates were still gazing out at her through the auditorium windows, looking shocked and annoyed by her outburst. Danielle Harrison was crying and pointing at her angrily. As Carrie raised a hand to brush some hair away from her face, she noticed that the mood ring was now changing color rapidly from the light blue of happiness to the purple of fear. At the same time, she found herself wondering whether Danielle and the rest of Lisa Jameson's offended friends might come after her. Her head spun.

"What do you think you were doing?" Mr. Wainwright asked furiously.

"I'm sorry. I just couldn't help it, sir," Carrie tried to explain.

"Lisa Jameson could have died last night, and all you can do is laugh," the teacher barked. "I'm surprised at you, Carrie. I thought you would have known better."

"Sir, I couldn't help it," Carrie insisted.

"You'll get a week's detention for that tasteless display of disrespect," he hissed. "Go to the detention room immediately. I don't think any of your teachers will want to see you today after that outburst. Your work will be brought to you. Go! Now!"

Carrie thought about trying to explain further but decided against it. She couldn't find the right words and, if she told Mr. Wainwright that she had actually been quite frightened by her own outburst, she knew he wouldn't believe her.

"And don't walk back through the auditorium," Mr. Wainwright added. "I think you've caused enough disturbance for one day. Walk around and through the school's main entrance. Maybe the fresh air will clear your head and make you realize how stupidly you've behaved."

Carrie did as she was told, trekking off along the path that ran around the perimeter of the school buildings until she reached the main entrance. She was beginning to feel angry with herself now. She walked in and headed straight for the detention room, slamming the door behind her in frustration.

She sat down at one of the desks near the back of the room, still furious that she had embarrassed herself so publicly. Carrie looked at the mood ring, expecting it to be red for the anger she was feeling.

But it was pink. The color of optimism!

What do I have to be optimistic about? Carrie wondered. *A week of detention? People in school hating me for laughing during the minute's silence? The possibility of Lisa Jameson's little gang coming after me?* She stared mutinously at the ring. The color was wrong. The ring was wrong. It was nothing but a stupid piece of junk!

In her anger, Carrie gripped the mood ring and tried to pull it off. It wouldn't budge. No matter how hard she tugged at it, the ring remained firmly on her right index finger.

This just made Carrie all the more furious, and yet, even as she watched, the stone in the ring turned orange — orange for contentment.

Carrie shook her head, her breathing a little ragged now. *This isn't right*, she thought. *Why won't the ring come off?* She felt nervous, as though there was a part of her she couldn't control — the part of her that had laughed in assembly even though she hadn't wanted to. For a few seconds, Carrie blamed the ring — even though she knew that was ridiculous.

She tried again to pull it free, and again it resisted her efforts. She swallowed hard and frowned at the mood ring. Then she heard footsteps heading toward the detention room and moments later, Mrs. Collins walked in, a furious expression on her face.

Despite the fact that she knew she was going to be told off again, Carrie was almost glad to see the principal. At least getting yelled at would take her mind off the ring for a while. And she was determined to take care of that, once and for all, when she got home.

You're late," said Carrie's mom as Carrie entered the house.

"I must be late if you're home before me," Carrie joked, wandering into the kitchen.

"She's late because she had detention," Mark smirked, looking up from the kitchen table where he was doing some homework.

"Why?" her mom asked. "What happened?"

"I'll tell you later," Carrie said. She headed straight for the sink and rubbed some soap on her index finger, working the slippery lather all around the mood ring. The stone was shining red for anger. *That just proves it doesn't work*, Carrie thought. *I'm not feeling angry at all.*

"My meeting finished early," her mom was saying. "So I thought I'd come home and cook dinner for a change."

Carrie nodded absently, her concentration focused on the ring. She began pulling at it, her finger now slippery with soap, but the irritating piece of jewelry remained stuck. She frowned in annoyance.

"What are you doing?" her mom asked curiously. "Can I help?"

"I can do it," Carrie snapped. Sighing in frustration, she wiped her hand on a paper towel and walked across to the table where Mark was sitting.

Without hesitation she dug her fingertip into the butter and spread the slippery mess around her finger, carefully getting it underneath the mood ring.

"That's sick," Mark said, watching her.

"Carrie, what are you trying to do?" Mrs. Peterson demanded.

"I'm trying to get this stupid ring off," Carrie retorted. "But it won't budge."

"Do you want me to try?" her mom asked.

"I said I can do it," Carrie blurted, feeling annoyed, but the ring remained on her finger as if welded there.

She wiped the butter off with a towel and hurried to the freezer, wrenching the door open.

"Now what?" Mark said, smiling.

"If my finger gets cold, it'll shrink," Carrie told him. "Then I'll be able to get the ring off."

"That's stupid," her mom said. "Now close the freezer door."

"Not until this ring's off," Carrie said defiantly. "I must get it off. I've *got* to."

"Carrie, you'll ruin the food that's in there. Close the door, please."

"Besides, your hand might get frostbite and drop off," Mark teased.

"Carrie, for goodness' sake, close the freezer door!" her mom insisted.

Carrie withdrew her hand and slammed the door in frustration. "I'm not being silly," she snapped. "I just want this ring to come off." She felt furious. Why couldn't her family understand how important it was for her to remove the ring? She was trapped, like an animal in a cage — except that there was no cage, just a tiny metal band around one finger. A tiny metal band that wouldn't come off.

She looked around wildly for something else that she might be able to use to free the ring. Her gaze fell on her mother's porcelain vase standing on top of the freezer.

"Honestly, Carrie," her mom was saying. "I don't know why you're making this into such a big deal. It's only a ring!"

Carrie felt like screaming. Instead, she snatched up the vase. "And this is just an ornament!" she yelled, throwing it across the room.

It hit the far wall and shattered into a dozen pieces

with a resounding *crash!* The silence that followed was deafening.

"That was my favorite vase," her mom said quietly. "Why did you do that?"

Carrie was already feeling guilty. Her anger had gone as quickly as it had come. She wanted to explain, but she didn't understand what was going on. She felt dizzy. Her head was full of conflicting thoughts. What was happening to her?

She looked at the horrified faces of her mother and brother. "Mom . . ." she began, feeling drained of energy.

"Clean up that mess, please," her mom said, a little sadly. "Then I think you should go to your room and think about what you've done. All this drama just because you can't get a ring off your finger. You're acting like a spoiled child!"

"I couldn't help it," Carrie said pitifully. "I don't know what's wrong. I've never had mood swings like this before."

Her mom merely nodded and continued making dinner.

Carrie crossed to the other side of the room, where the broken pieces of the vase lay scattered across the floor. She bent slowly and reached for the first piece.

As she stretched out her hand, she saw that the mood ring had changed color again. It was yellow now. The color of sickness. Instinctively, Carrie put one hand to her forehead, but she didn't seem to have a temperature. She wasn't ill. At least, she didn't think she was, and yet, as she pulled her shaking hand away, she saw that her skin was covered in a sheen of sweat.

She felt suddenly weak, and it seemed as if every muscle in her body ached. Her mouth filled with bile, and she realized that she was going to be sick. Carrie jumped to her feet and ran for the downstairs bathroom.

She made it to the sink and leaned her head forward. Gasping for breath, she felt her stomach clenching like a fist, but nothing came up. She wiped her mouth with the back of her hand, her mind reeling. Sweat was pouring down her face, yet she felt as cold as ice. "Carrie," her mom said, appearing in the doorway, looking anxious.

Carrie nodded, unable to speak.

"Come on," her mom said gently, trying to help her up. "I didn't realize you were sick. Go on up to bed."

Carrie waved away her mother's help. "I can manage, thanks, Mom," she gasped, relieved that her stomach seemed to be settling.

"Just go and rest," her mom said. "I'll bring you some ginger ale in a minute."

"I just need to lie down for a moment," Carrie replied. "I'll come down when I feel better." She put out a hand to get to her feet and saw that the ring was light blue — for happiness!

Now what? Carrie wondered.

She climbed the stairs slowly, aware that her mom was still standing in the hallway watching her. She was halfway up when the corners of her mouth began to lift in the same way they had that morning at school. As soon as the smile began to spread across her face, she immediately hurried up to her room and shut the door behind her so her mom wouldn't see.

She jumped onto her bed and buried her face in the pillow to muffle the laughter that was now beginning to spill from her — laughter over which she had no control.

For several minutes, she lay there, laughing, until finally the hysterics began to subside. She sat up and looked at the ring. There had been the incident in assembly that morning, then the furious outburst in the kitchen, followed by sickness, and now more uncontrollable laughter.

Don't even think it. It's impossible! Carrie told herself. But, no matter how impossible it seemed, she could think of only one explanation: The ring had shown the appropriate color just before each of the incidents had taken place. Instead of mirroring her moods, was the ring actually controlling them?

She shook her head, anxious to dismiss the ridiculous idea. But how else could she explain what had happened? Carrie sat on her bed, staring at the ring. Then she reached for her cell phone and entered her cousin Amy's number.

"Please be there, Amy," Carrie said under her breath, listening to the phone ring.

"Hello?"

"Amy, it's me," Carrie told her. "I need to tell you something. I know it's going to sound crazy, but please just listen."

When Carrie finally finished telling her cousin everything that had happened since she'd acquired the mood ring, there was nothing but silence on the other end of the phone.

"Amy, are you still there?" Carrie asked frantically.

"Yes, I'm just trying to figure out what's going on," Amy replied. "So you think that the ring isn't reflecting your moods, it's creating them, right? You think the ring's controlling you?"

"I know it sounds insane, but I don't know what else to think," Carrie responded.

"It came off the front of a magazine you bought for five dollars, Carrie. How powerful can it be?" Amy said.

"I knew you wouldn't believe me," Carrie said, sighing.

"I didn't say that. I just think it's a little, well, far-fetched, that's all," Amy told her.

"So do I, but I don't know how else to explain what's been happening to me. And, like I said, I can't get the stupid thing off!"

"Maybe the best person to ask would be the old woman who ran the stall where you bought the magazine," Amy suggested.

"But she doesn't even know I've got the ring," Carrie pointed out.

"Well, go to the market and tell her. Talk to her. She might know something about it."

"You think I'm crazy, don't you, Amy?" Carrie asked.

"No. I think you're scared and confused," Amy replied. "And I think you should go and talk to the old woman, Carrie. The market's open today. I bet she'll be there. Call me again after you've spoken to her."

Carrie took a deep breath. "Thanks, Amy," she said quietly, and hung up.

She pulled on a jacket and edged slowly out of her room. She could hear voices coming from the kitchen, and she knew that if she was going to get to the park she would have to sneak out of the house. Her mom would never let her out when she was sick.

Carrie crept quietly down the stairs, paused at the bottom, then tiptoed to the front door. She slipped out and closed the door as quietly as possible behind her, then she sprinted down the street. Instantly, she felt a little better. If the ring was dictating her moods, she was better off away from her family. If it made her angry again, she was afraid of what she might do.

She ran faster, aware that the market would be closing soon. She didn't want to miss the old woman who had sold her the magazine. As she ran, she felt her index finger throbbing, as if the ring was tightening its grip.

Carrie ran on, hurtling across the road without looking to see if there was any traffic coming. She felt herself shiver and wondered, for one terrible moment, if she was going to throw up after all. She looked down at the ring. It was changing swiftly from yellow to brown. Just as rapidly, she felt confusion fill her head and, for a few seconds, she couldn't remember the way to the park. She skidded to a halt on a street corner and looked around in bewilderment. The feeling passed as the ring turned to light blue, and Carrie continued running.

There were some little children playing across the street. Carrie she saw one of them fall and land heavily on the pavement. He started to cry as his friends gathered around him, but Carrie could only laugh out loud at the sight.

At last, she reached the park and dashed through the gates. The market was still open, so Carrie ran toward the site of the stall where she'd bought the magazine, but there was no sign of the old woman! Carrie looked around frantically, then hurried across to the stall opposite. There was a man there selling used clothes. He was packing up.

"Excuse me," Carrie said. "Has the lady who sells books and magazines been here today?"

The man shrugged. "I guess so," he said vaguely.

"You must have seen her," Carrie snapped.

"Who do you mean?" he asked.

"She's old. She runs a stall that sells used books and vintage magazines."

"There's a couple of stalls like that here," he replied unhelpfully.

"She means Four-fingered Lily," said a man selling toys and games at a neighboring stall. He looked at Carrie. "Don't you, Miss?"

"Is that her name?" Carrie asked.

He nodded. "She's been coming here for years," the man said. "Longer than I have, I suppose."

"Do you know where she is? I need to speak to her," Carrie begged.

"You just missed her. She packed up about five minutes ago."

"Which way did she go?" Carrie demanded frantically. "Please tell me."

The man nodded toward the park's other entrance.

Carrie was about to turn and run in that direction when a thought struck her. "Why is she called that?" she asked him. "Four-fingered Lily?"

"Because she's missing a finger!" he said with a smile. "Why else?"

Carrie took off as fast as she could. She scanned the pathways of the park — and suddenly spotted a figure pushing a shopping cart full of cardboard boxes. She ran toward the old woman and caught up with her at last.

"I have to speak to you," Carrie said, panting.

"What about?" the old woman asked, still pushing the shopping cart.

"About this," Carrie said, raising her right index finger and brandishing it in front of the old lady like a weapon.

"You said you wanted it, but I wouldn't let you have it!" the old lady exclaimed, stopping in surprise. "Where did you get it from?"

"I found it on the ground," Carrie told her. "But you

knew about it, didn't you? That's why you didn't want me to have it."

"Girls! They can never resist a pretty piece of jewelry. I was the same when I was your age," said the old lady, shaking her head. Suddenly, she spun around to face Carrie, pulling her own right hand from inside her coat pocket and holding it out.

Carrie stared. The index finger of the old lady's right hand was missing. There was little more than a stump where the digit should have been.

"I was like you," said the woman. "I saw a mood ring and I wanted it and I got it. Along with things I didn't want. That was why I got rid of it." She tapped the stump of her index finger. "The trouble was, I couldn't take off the ring." She thrust the stump toward Carrie. "This was the only way to get rid of the ring. And if you've got any sense, you'll do the same. Before it's too late," she finished, pushing her shopping cart again.

"What do you mean 'before it's too late'?" Carrie called after her.

"You already know what I mean," the old lady said over her shoulder. "You know what must be done."

Carrie stood alone, watching as the old lady walked away. For a moment, she feared she was going to pass out, but the feeling subsided. Returning home, she went a little slower this time, not sure what she was going to say when she got back. How was she going to explain to her mom and dad what she'd just heard? They would never believe her about the ring.

As Carrie walked, the old lady's words echoed inside her head: *You know what must be done.*

Where have you been? I thought you were sick. You were supposed to be resting in your room!" Mrs. Peterson said as Carrie walked into the house.

Carrie burst into tears. It happened so suddenly even she was surprised. She ran to her mom, who threw both arms around her and hugged her.

"What's wrong, sweetheart?" her mom asked.

"I've got to get this ring off, Mom." Carrie sobbed, holding up her right index finger.

"I don't blame you, it's a tacky piece of jewelry," Mrs. Peterson remarked.

"No, you don't understand. It's been doing things

to me. Making me feel things I don't want to feel. Making me *act* in ways I don't want to act."

"Don't be silly, honey. It's just a ring," her mom said firmly.

"Just help me get it off. *Please!*" Carrie shrieked. "There's something wrong with it."

Mrs. Peterson shook her head. "You can be such a drama queen at times," she said, stroking Carrie's hair. "But, come on, if I can help you get that silly old ring off, I will." She led Carrie into the kitchen just as the phone rang in the living room. Mrs. Peterson gave Carrie a hug and went to answer it.

You know what must be done. Carrie heard the old woman's voice in her head. *Before it's too late.*

Still sobbing, she looked down at the ring. It was yellow for sickness. She felt a stabbing pain in her stomach and looked around frantically for something to help her get the ring off. She could see nothing she hadn't already tried, so she gripped the ring and twisted it on her finger, desperate to remove it.

She got it as far as the knuckle, twisting and pulling at it until her skin was red and sore. She continued to tug at it despite the pain, but it would go no farther. Carrie tried once more, the edge of the ring actually cutting into her flesh.

You know what must be done.

Carrie was crying as she pulled open the kitchen drawer and grabbed the largest, sharpest knife. She placed it on the table and sat down. The ring glowed purple.

Blinking away her tears, she stared at the knife but didn't touch it. She wondered if she could do what needed to be done and began imagining what it would be like to have only four fingers on her right hand. Soon, she was sobbing so hard that she couldn't even focus her eyes on the knife.

The mood ring was still purple.

Carrie took a deep breath. She stared at the knife, unable to lift her hand.

Do it! Before it's too late! she thought.

"NO!" Mrs. Peterson screamed, racing into the kitchen and knocking the knife off the table. "What are you doing?" her mother shrieked.

The knife skittered across the floor and Mrs.

Peterson lunged for it. "Carrie!" she shouted. "What were you thinking?"

Carrie just stared. The ring glowed even more yellow than before. And then Carrie slipped into unconsciousness.

The light was blinding. So white and bright in its intensity that Carrie could barely open her eyes. When she finally did, she saw that the walls of the room she was in were the same bright white. So was the bed linen and the long nightgown that she wore. She swung herself out of bed and took a couple of steps across the room.

She tried to remember what had happened. In her mind's eye, she saw herself sitting at the kitchen table, and she saw her mother trying to grab something. . . .

The memories flooded back. She looked down at her right hand. The ring was still there on her index finger. It showed light blue. Happiness.

Carrie felt her face break into a smile, but it was a gesture over which she had absolutely no control. She didn't feel happy, far from it, but her smile wouldn't fade. Not even when she got to her feet, walked over to the cold metal door, and pulled at the handle — only to find that it wouldn't open. It was locked.

There was a small opening in the door that looked like a mail slot with glass across it. She peered through the slot, then stepped back hurriedly as some people approached and unlocked the door.

She didn't recognize the man in the white coat who walked in first. Her parents followed him into the room, looking upset and anxious. Carrie wanted to get up and run to them, but she didn't move.

"Carrie," the doctor said softly.

She began to laugh. A high-pitched, frenzied laugh that she couldn't suppress.

"It's the same every time we speak to her," the man told her parents. "We can't get a word out of her. She's been like this ever since she was brought in to the hospital. I've worked in psychiatry for twelve years now, and I've never seen a case quite like this one."

Carrie opened her mouth to speak, annoyed that the man was talking about her as if she wasn't there. She wanted to tell her mom and dad how much she loved them. She wanted them to take her away from this strange white place. But she couldn't. She could only laugh, the infernal sound reverberating off the walls, mocking and spiteful. The only sound Carrie could make. The only sound she would ever hear. Now — and for the rest of her life.